A NEXT GENERATION NOVEL

TEMPT Us

J.M. WALKER

IBSN: 978-1-989782-50-7

Tempt Us (Next Generation, #11)

FAMILY TREE

Angel and Genevieve "Jay" Rodriguez
(Grit, King's Harlots #1/Grim, King's Harlots #3)
Angelica "Gigi"
Ryder
Meadow

Asher and Meeka Donovan
(Stain, King's Harlots #2)
Aiden
Ashton

Coby and Brogan Porter
(Rude, King's Harlots #4/For You, King's Harlots #7)
Zachary "Zach"

Dale and Maxine "Max" Michaels
(Numb, King's Harlots #5)
Piper

Vincent "Stone" and Creena Stone
(Rust, King's Harlots #6)
Luna
Vincent Junior

Greyson and Eve Mercer
(Greyson, Hell's Harlem #1)
Jaron

Tray and Zillah Lister
(Tray, Hell's Harlem #2)
Beatrix "Bee"

John and Beatrix "Trixie" Butcher
(Hell's Harlem Series)
Cyrus
Samson "Sammy"

WARNING

Please be advised that this book does deal with alcoholism. It's mentioned quite a bit throughout the book, so if that's a trigger for you, please read with caution.

DEDICATION

To Aiden.
It's been a long road but your story is finally
being told.

PROLOGUE

AIDEN

SMOKE BILLOWED AROUND ME. It steamed from the hood of my car, proving how much I fucked up. How I always fuck up.

No matter how much I thought I was taking a step forward, something always sets me back. It was inevitable. I was a failure.

I should leave.

I should get out of this place before I was found. Before I was caught doing whatever it was I had been doing for what felt like eternity.

I racked my brain for answers. To try and figure out what I had done a couple of hours ago, only to end up in this place.

In this hell.

It wasn't a hell you could see or even touch. But one you could feel. It was constantly with me.

Holding me.

Consuming me.

It was everywhere.

No matter where I went, it was there. Taking the very control from me I never wanted to give anyone.

Ever.

Flashing red and blue lights burned into my eyes. They were almost hypnotizing, putting me in a trance as I waited for that darkness to consume me.

Take me. Please take me.

I wasn't sure what was going on, but I did know it was late at night. Or early in the morning. Depending on how you looked at it.

It was almost like life in a way. You either looked at it as the glass being half full or the glass being half empty. I was always the latter. Not at first. Not until I was taken away because of a job, only to come back broken, destroyed, and less of the man I once was.

My mom noticed first. She asked me often how I was doing. How could I tell her that I just didn't know? People didn't understand when you couldn't figure out what was wrong or put a label on it.

Post-traumatic stress disorder.

It was a thing. A very serious thing. And I knew before I stepped foot back on American soil, I had it.

I was in the Navy for just over a year. Longer if you counted the weeks I spent in basic training. Getting deployed as soon as I was able to made my father and his fellow Navy brothers proud. But it ended quickly and I had been falling into myself ever since.

People noticed.

My friends noticed.

I noticed.

But there was not a damn thing I could do about it. I needed help and I didn't know how to ask for it.

Everything around me was like it had come right out of a movie. There was smoke. A whole lot of smoke. Flashing lights. People milling about. Some were dressed in uniforms while others wore regular clothes. Had I been in an accident?

I did a mental scan of my body and wasn't sure exactly what I was feeling or not. I was numb, closed off even and I couldn't figure out why.

What happened?

I thought back to earlier that night. I had gone to a bar to drown out my sorrows while I continued feeling sorry for myself.

Words, hateful, god-awful words were said earlier that evening but from who? I had gotten into a fight with someone. The area around my eye stung, almost like that thought reminded me that I had been hit but I couldn't remember by who.

"You ever talk to your mother like that again, I'll slam your head through the fucking wall." Cold angry eyes that matched my own, glared at me. "You know what? I'm sick of this shit. I don't want to see you again until you can man up and take care of your damn issues."

The memory hit me, forcing all air from my lungs.

I had gotten into a fight with my dad.

I remembered it now. It all started coming back to me.

A sour taste filled my throat as I remembered downing a bottle of whatever it was I could get my hands on earlier that afternoon. Or maybe it was the day before. Time was lost on me as I tried thinking through the gamut of shitty things I had done over the past few months. Who was I fucking kidding? It was longer than months. It had even been longer than a year of me being in a bad mood and taking it out on those who loved me.

I needed help but I didn't know how to ask for it.

I needed time but couldn't grasp it.

I needed something. A change. To get out of this town. To go somewhere. Anywhere.

Anywhere that wasn't here.

Cool air suddenly fanned over my face.

"Sir? We're going to get you out." The man, whoever he was, was fuzzy in my vision. I couldn't make him out, but I saw that he was big, dressed in a uniform. I couldn't focus. Maybe I should just go to sleep. Then I wouldn't fight with my parents. I wouldn't be a disappointment and a constant reminder to them that one of their sons was a fuck-up.

Maybe I should just go.

Maybe I should just stay.

Maybe I should tell them what was wrong with me even though I had never put it into words. I spent so long forgetting what happened that the moment I tried thinking of it, my hand reached for a bottle.

I wanted to drown.

I was vaguely aware of being pulled from the car. Every inch of me tingled but there were parts I still couldn't feel. I just felt... *numb*.

I was unaware of what happened. If I crashed. If I hurt myself or worse, someone else. The only thing I knew at that moment, was that I needed something. Before I killed myself or an innocent person. Until then, I wasn't sure how I would cope but I had to figure it out.

Even if I died trying.

ONE

AIDEN

LEANING MY ARMS ON the bar top, I stared at the pint of beer in front of me like I was expecting it to drink itself, or move, or do some fancy trick I wasn't prepared for. The bubbles in the golden liquid popped and danced, teasing me until I took that sip that would bring me down a dark and dangerous road. It was one I had been down more times than I cared to admit.

My eyes flicked to the shot glass sitting beside the pint. Both were still full. Both could destroy me if I let them. Maybe I should. Then it would at least drown out the noises in my head. The constant chatter was enough to drive anyone to drink.

The noises weren't even memories anymore. They were little voices telling me that I was a failure. I would never amount to anything. My parents would never forgive me. Constant reminders that I didn't deserve happiness.

I was vaguely aware of someone sitting on the stool right beside me. Couldn't they see that there was more space in this establishment? Why the hell did they have to sit so close? I rubbed the back of my neck, trying to ease some of the tension scraping along my skin. Even my inner voice was an asshole.

"You going to drink those or just stare at them all night?"

The deep voice pulled my gaze to the left. The person sitting directly beside me was a man. A very good-looking man I might add.

Strong jaw with light stubble, piercing light blue eyes, and brown crew cut hair. He looked to be about my height or maybe a little taller than my six-four. He was wide in the shoulders. I wondered what it would feel like to be held by him. The thought was sudden and one I wasn't prepared for.

The back of my neck heated but thankfully, the stranger didn't seem to notice.

Instead of answering him, I signaled the bartender.

She came over instantly, giving me a wide smile. Her dark brown eyes roamed over me, her tongue licking along her teeth. "What can I get for you, handsome?" she purred. She must have been new because the female staff at this bar knew I was never interested.

"A bottle of water please," I said, pushing the shot glass and pint a couple of inches back.

"You want me to take those?" Her eyes dropped to the drinks in front of me that were still full.

"Yeah, sure." I pushed them farther away from me, itching to take them back just the same. I could have them gone in less than a minute, but something was different about tonight. As much as I wanted those drinks, I realized that I didn't actually *need* them. Not like before. Not like I used to. Was this it? Was I finally moving forward? No. My jaw clenched. A thought hit me so fast, it practically slapped me in the face. I didn't need these drinks. I needed a fucking bottle.

I had been attending AA meetings for awhile now but I never thought they did anything. I went, and listened, and left.

But something in the air on this cool evening, told me not to have a drink.

The bartender hesitated but took the drinks and dumped them out in the sink. "You still have to pay for them."

"I figured."

"Did you want anything else?" she asked, placing a bottle of water in front of me and licking her lips.

I bit back an eyeroll.

My mom taught me to be nice and polite but no matter how much I stated that I wasn't attracted to this woman, she would still get offended. Probably wonder what it was about her I didn't like. Maybe complain to her friends later about the man at the bar who wouldn't give her the time of day.

"Just water is fine," I murmured, picking at a random fuzz on my ripped jeans. "For now, anyway."

She huffed, finally getting the hint, and went back to serving other customers.

I bit back a chuckle, shaking my head.

"I'm surprised she didn't start humping your leg," the guy beside me mumbled. "People will never learn."

I grunted, almost forgetting he was there. Or that was what I tried telling myself. Truth was, I could feel him. His presence set my senses on overdrive. It was definitely a new feeling for me and one that I wanted to explore. "Apparently."

"So, why are you drinking alone on a Tuesday night?"

My head slowly turned, my eyes connecting with his. "Do you always ask random strangers why they're drinking alone on a Tuesday night?"

His full mouth pulled at the corners, turning up into a wide grin. "Not usually but better late than never, right?"

A laugh bubbled from me, surprising myself. The sound had been so foreign to my ears, I almost forgot what it sounded like leaving my mouth.

His grin widened. "I thought it sounded good."

My laughter subsided, unleashing this light feeling on my shoulders. It was almost like at that single moment, that laughter with this mysterious stranger I didn't know, lifted some of the heaviness from my body.

"Are you from around here?" I heard myself ask, taking a sip of my water.

"I am but I don't usually end up in this part of the city." He sighed, taking a swig from his own water bottle. "I work from home and being stuck inside four walls day in and day out is enough to drive a person mad."

"But you took it even further and left your area," I reminded him. "You must really hate your job."

"Yeah, my boss is a dick." He winked, signaling the bartender over. "Can I get another water please and a Bloody Mary but without any alcohol in it?"

The bartender narrowed her brows at him. "You don't want any alcohol in it?" She rolled her eyes. "Why not?"

The hackles on the back of my neck rose.

"It's actually none of your business why I don't want any alcohol in my drink and if you don't start fixing up your attitude, I'll contact your manager and have you fired in less than two point five seconds." He lifted his hand, staring down at his wrist. "One." He looked up. "Two," he counted even though he wasn't actually wearing a watch.

The bartender huffed, blowing a loose strand of hair out of her eyes. "You don't have to be—"

"Point five." He picked his phone up off the bar top, pressed a button and lifted it to his ear. "Hey, it's Rowan. Your bartender just quit. I don't know. She went to say something about how she—"

The bartender placed a drink in front of him.

"Never mind. She was kidding." He hung up the phone and placed it back on the bar top in front of him. "Was that so hard?"

"I didn't know that you knew my boss," she mumbled.

"I don't," the man who I now knew as Rowan, said, taking a sip of what I could only assume was his virgin Bloody Mary. He met my gaze. "Did you want one? It's pretty good."

"Uh…sure. Can you make mine a virgin one too please?" I asked the bartender.

She rolled her eyes again but went about making my drink.

"It's Rowan."

My head whipped around. "I'm sorry?"

"Rowan," he repeated. "It's my name. Rowan Crane."

"Oh, I assumed so when you told whoever was on the phone that you were Rowan." I lifted my water bottle. "Aiden Donovan."

"Touché." He chuckled, clinking his glass against my plastic bottle. "Nice to meet you, Aiden."

"Nice to meet you too."

The bartender brought my drink over and left shortly after, only to be replaced by another woman. This one looked to be a little older. She smiled at us, looked down at our drinks that were still quite full, and went about making orders for other customers.

"So do you actually know the boss here or were you telling her the truth when you said that you don't?" I asked Rowan, curious about the man who had suddenly invaded my evening.

"I don't know him technically. I just did some computer work for him. But she doesn't need to know that." He shrugged like it was no big deal and maybe it wasn't.

"Well thank you for…" When my voice trailed off, I realized that I wasn't even sure what I wanted to thank him for.

"Don't worry about it. My parents aren't drinkers, and they always have issues whenever we go out to dinner. It's like people expect everyone to have a drink. It's stupid."

I nodded, swirling the straw around and around in the glass tumbler. "Alcohol is dangerous. For me anyway." And why the hell would I tell him that? A complete stranger who probably didn't even give two shits as to why I didn't drink.

Smooth, Aiden. Real fucking smooth.

Taking a sip of the Bloody Mary, a part of me longed for alcohol. But it had caused me problems already, lots of problems, so there was no way I could have another drop of it. At the same time, it had never stopped me before. It was a constant battle. A should I or shouldn't I situation that I would probably never be able to conquer. I would try. It was all I could do. I almost lost my life as a result of this addiction. I couldn't go through that again, but I especially couldn't put my parents through that hell.

"Alcohol can be very dangerous," Rowan said gently, his deep voice pulling me from my thoughts. "Some people are lucky enough that they can have a social drink and stop. Others are on the cusp of being an alcoholic and don't even realize it. And then there are those people who can't do anything else but have that drink. It controls them."

"And makes them, and everyone around them, miserable," I muttered.

"Yeah." Rowan turned toward me.

I could feel his eyes burning into the side of my head, but I couldn't look at him for fear that he would see all of my truths hidden within me. Most of those truths I didn't even know about myself.

"Did you want to grab a booth?"

I looked at him then. "Why?"

"Because it's more comfortable." He tilted his head. "Is that a problem?"

"No." I gave myself a shake. "Sorry, it's been a long…well, it doesn't matter. But sure…I'd love to get a booth."

He nodded, blowing out a slow breath like he could only move on if I said yes. I wasn't sure why or even how but there was something about Rowan Crane that I found I needed. I didn't know what that was but either way, whatever we were doing, I realized that I liked it.

TWO

ROWAN

HE WAS SAD.

Before I approached Aiden, I could sense the heavy emotions seeping off of him like added weights. I had seen the same in my father. It took my mother to bring him down. She was his safe space and I prayed that I could one day be the same for someone else if it was needed.

A part of me felt sorry for Aiden, while another part was drawn to him in ways I had never experienced or understood. I spent countless hours upon hours researching all different types of sexualities because I had thought something was wrong with me at first when it wasn't just women I had been attracted to. Hell, it wasn't even just men I was drawn to either.

I was fascinated by everyone.

Literally.

I didn't care what you had between your legs or what you identified as.

Through the years, I learned that I was pansexual. But now that I was getting older, casual sex just didn't do it for me anymore.

Aiden had been the first person in years I had approached at a bar. There was definitely something in him that called out to me. I wanted to wrap him up in my arms and just hold him and keep him safe. Which again, wasn't normal for me either.

After I asked him if he wanted to grab a booth, it was almost like I could see a wall go up. He was protecting himself and I wasn't sure why. We didn't know each other, which was fine, it was how a lot of relationships started, but he didn't need to second-guess anything when it came to me. I was honest and said anything that was on my mind. I got that trait from both of my parents. As long as you treated me well, I would do the same in return.

When we had moved from the bar to the booth, I noticed how Aiden almost melted into the seat. He let out a sigh, his shoulders slumping and his eyes closing for just a moment. When they opened, they landed on me. He gave me a small smile, his cheeks turning a nice shade of pink.

A thought came to me.

Him on his knees, looking up at me.

Waiting. Wanting. *Needing.*

A shiver raced down my spine at the mere idea of him submitting to me.

While Aiden played with the straw in his drink, I couldn't help but watch him. He was blond with lightly tanned skin. He appeared to be in shape but a little on the skinny side. Bags sat under his eyes, a light scruff covering his strong jaw. It made me wonder if something had happened and if he had lost some weight as a result of it.

Aiden continued twirling the straw around in his drink, looking out at the vast space of the bar area while I watched him. His blond hair was a little longer on top. His jaw was angular, strong and sure, while a muscle ticked just beneath his ear. His eyes were a light shade of blue but held pain I had seen before in those closest to me.

As much as I wanted to hear his voice and actually learn more about him, I found that I liked the silence just the same. It was comfortable and needed, all the while a little confusing too.

"Did you want to order something to eat?" I heard myself ask.

His head slowly turned, his gaze connecting with mine. "Sure."

"Are you allergic to anything?" I asked him, picking the menu up off the table between us.

"No. I'll eat anything really." He gave me a small smile then, and though he had smiled before, this one actually reached his eyes.

My dick twitched, pushing against the fly of my jeans.

I never realized that a simple smile could turn me on until Aiden did it.

Clearing my throat, I looked over the menu and ended up ordering us a plate of nachos because you couldn't really go wrong with them. While we waited for our food, I sat back on my side of the booth and took a sip from my drink.

"What do you do for a living?" he asked, following suit and taking a sip of his drink as well.

"I own an antique store." It was on the tip of my tongue to tell him what I really did. While I did have an actual store, it was a cover. What actually paid the bills, was helping people get information. And it wasn't always done the legal way.

"Oh! I would like to see it one day," he blurted, snapping his mouth shut. "I mean…I just…"

"Hey." I leaned forward and reached across the table, placing a hand on his arm. "I'd love to show you my store. There's something there for everyone. I've been collecting things for years. Some people have even donated items. I have books older than dirt, model airplanes that go way back, and more. I think you'd like it." But how the hell would I know if he would like it or not? This guy, this stranger, had me unravelled.

His eyes dropped to my hand resting on his arm a little too long for it to be just considered a nice gesture.

I pulled my hand back, already missing his warmth. "I'm sorry."

"Don't be." He shook his head. "I've never done this before, so…"

"What? Have drinks with a guy?" It was meant to tease but truth was, I wasn't sure if he was into women, men, both, or nothing at all. I didn't want to overstep but at the same time, I wanted to crowd his space and have him just focus on me. Fuck me, it had been way too long since I went home with someone, I was lusting after a damn stranger.

"With anyone really." He placed his drink back on the table in front of him. "I don't really date and any time I did date, was only because I felt I had to. My friends are now married with kids. My brother, who was the biggest lady's man I know, has even settled down."

"You want more," I added, soaking up Aiden's words like a damn sponge.

He nodded, brushing his blond bangs out of his eyes. "I do or I think I do anyway. I just want a friend really."

"Same here," I told him, not wanting him to feel alone. "My sister is married and has two boys. My nephews are the best kids I know but I could be a little biased."

He chuckled, brushing his bangs away again. I realized he did that whenever he was nervous but there was no reason for him to be. Not around me anyway.

"I would also love a friend. Someone I can shoot the shit with. Someone I can call up in the middle of the night because I need to talk to them. Sure, I have acquaintances, like most of us do I imagine. But I don't have a best friend."

Aiden picked up a napkin off the table between us and started ripping it into small pieces. "My brother is my best friend but even he doesn't know me completely. Not for lack of trying on his part anyway."

I wanted to ask him more and find out every single thing that made him tick but when our nachos came, the words died on my tongue.

We ate in a comfortable silence. It was a silence I had never been used to before. If I ever went out on a date, it was usually with women, sometimes a guy slipped in, but not often. Whomever it was with though, always talked or wanted me to talk. Sure, if we were friends, I could chat your ear off like the best of them but until that happened, I was an observer. I listened before speaking.

It was on the tip of my tongue to ask who he was attracted to, but something told me that maybe he wasn't sure.

"What do *you* do for a living?" I asked once we were picking at the last few bits and pieces of the nachos.

A dark shadow passed over Aiden's face, but it had disappeared as quickly as it had arrived. "I own a construction company with my brother. It belonged to a friend of our father's, and he took over after his friend retired. But now that Dad's retired too, he left it to me and Ashton." He cleared his throat. "I was also in the Navy for a short time," he muttered, his voice soft.

"But you aren't anymore?" I asked, my heart jumping at the sudden nervous energy coming off of him.

"No. It's a long story and one I don't want to bore you with."

I wanted to ask him what happened and to tell him that he could never bore me, but I didn't. Those words never fell from my lips because one, I didn't know him, and two, I didn't want to do anything that could jeopardize this newfound friendship I suddenly wanted with him.

The waitress came back around and asked if we wanted anything else. I told her no and asked for the check. I noticed then how Aiden's shoulders seemed to drop a little, like he didn't want this night to end. Or maybe I had imagined it because I was the one who didn't want it to end yet.

When the waitress returned with the bill, I quickly took it from her.

Aiden's eyes widened a bit. "Let me pay."

"No." I took some cash from my wallet and placed it on the table. "It's my treat, since I kind of forced myself on you and made you eat with me."

"You didn't force anything on me. I liked…I liked this." He shrugged.

My heart skipped a beat.

"I insist," was all I said.

"Well, thank you. I'll pay next time."

Our eyes locked. When he realized what he had said, his cheeks turned an even darker shade of red. It was a nice color on him and one I wanted to put there often.

"If you want to hang out again," he added, trying to backtrack. "I shouldn't have assumed."

"Assume away." Because I *did* want to hang out with him. I wanted to find out all of his deepest and darkest secrets, what he was attracted to and whether or not he could be attracted to me in return.

He slid from the booth, shoving his hands in the pockets of his jeans.

I did the same and was about to set up something so there could be a next time, when my phone started ringing. "Sorry." I fished my phone out of my pocket and saw that it was my mom calling me. "It's my mom."

Aiden nodded and began walking to the front door of the bar.

I answered the phone and followed him. "Hey, Mama. What's up?"

"Hey, sweetheart. You free Thursday night for dinner?"

"Aren't we meeting up on Sunday?" It had been a regular thing ever since both my sister and I had moved out on our own.

"Usually yes but your father wants to take me away for the weekend, so we thought we'd do dinner on Thursday instead."

"I'm sure I can move things around to make time for you."

"Ha." She laughed. "You're funny."

I chuckled. "I can definitely be there."

"Good." She paused. "You on a date?"

My stomach did a flip. "No, I'm not on a date."

Aiden looked at me then, something flashing behind his eyes.

"I did make a new friend though," I told her, not taking my gaze from his.

His full mouth pulled up into a smile and I now understood what my dad meant when he said that he always worked to keep a smile on my mom's face. Seeing Aiden smile was something I now would make a mission for him to do every time I saw him.

"Oh, that's good. Friends are always good. We can never have too many of them."

I agreed with her there but most of my friends, and I used that term loosely, weren't actual friends and were only there when they or I, needed something.

"Well, I'll let you go," Mom continued. "See you Thursday."

We said our goodbyes and I disconnected the call. "Sorry about that. My family usually gets together every Sunday for dinner, but my parents are apparently going away this weekend, so dinner has been bumped up."

"That's nice," Aiden said, a faraway gaze appearing on his face. He cleared his throat, gave himself a shake and started backing up. "Well, it was nice meeting you, Rowan. Thank you for the drink and nachos." Before I could say anything more, he turned and rushed off.

I went to follow him to ask for his number, but my phone rang again. "Yeah," I answered.

"I miss you," came a deep voice from the other end.

My stomach sunk.

When I turned to follow Aiden, he had disappeared. I didn't know where he had gone. This attraction I had for him was short-lived because I wasn't sure if I would ever see him again.

THREE

AIDEN

It had been a few days since I met Rowan and what sucked about it was that I never got his phone number. Which was funny in a way when I had never wanted to get another person's number before.

All of the people I had slept with had only been because of my brother setting it up or because I was hit on and I felt like it had been the right thing to do. I was confused, messed up even, and I didn't know how to fix it.

Fix *me*.

I had no one I could talk to. No one who knew how I felt or who would just listen and not try to give me their opinions. I didn't want opinions or advice. I just wanted someone who would offer the comfort of their silence.

I had gone back to the bar the night before, but Rowan never showed up. I ordered a Bloody Mary because I had been thinking about him and hoped that maybe by having the same drink, it would somehow conjure him up out of nowhere. But of course, that never happened.

After being hit on again by the same bartender from the other night, I moved to a different section of the bar where she wasn't serving and ordered a plate of nachos.

I could have asked the owner of the bar if he knew anything about Rowan and how I could contact him, but I didn't.

One day, about a week later, I made my way into a library that was a block away from the bar where I'd met Rowan. I had every intention of sitting at one of the tables and reading. It was a hobby I picked up recently and one I wished I would have ventured into a long time ago. Reading other people's words and the worlds these authors built, brought me out of my head. If I could truly focus, I could spend hours at the library. On days where I had a hard time getting out of my head, I would just take out a few books and read them at home.

Before I could make my way to the stacks and rows of books, my eyes jumped to a bulletin board. Wanted ads were pinned to it, along with a few pictures of missing cats and dogs. Babysitting services littered the bottom of the board, along with other job offers as well. I was surprised to see all of them when most people resorted to using social media.

My eyes landed on an apartment ad. The person was asking for a roommate. I never wanted to move out of the apartment I shared with my brother for years but since he met his wife and moved out, I had been lonely and hardly stayed at home anyway. A change in scenery could be good for me.

Ashton and Tabatha had lived with me for a while but over time, I had insisted that they find their own place. They did and even made up a room for me. I appreciated it but I never stayed with them. It made me feel like I was a burden or that they pitied me and that was the only reason they set up the room in the first place.

The apartment held too many memories that I didn't want to think of but had no one to tell that to. Not even the people at my AA meetings knew about how I would rather waste money and sleep at a motel, than my own bed.

I unpinned the ad from the board and typed the address into my phone. The phone number listed was followed by a name.

Ro.

I frowned, Rowan suddenly making an appearance at the forefront of my mind. There was no way it was the same person. It was just a coincidence. Life couldn't be that nice to me. My stomach twisted. I still wished I would have gotten the guy's number.

Calling up the number, a deep voice answered after the first ring.

"Um…hi. I found the ad you left at a library about three blocks from your address. I was wondering if you're still looking for a roommate." I waited but when no response came, I thought for sure the guy had hung up.

"I have time now, if you're wanting to come look at the place," the guy finally said.

"Yes please, I do." It looked like I would be making an appearance and changing some things sooner than I would have thought possible.

We said our goodbyes and I hailed a taxi. I gave the driver the address and made my way to what I would hope, could be my new home. I needed a change and while it wasn't overly safe to make drastic choices at moment's notice, I needed something else besides the apartment I had once shared with my brother.

When the taxi stopped in front of a high-rise, I paid and left the vehicle. I mentally gave myself a pep talk and said that I could do this. I could make a change and be a better person. I had this.

Once I was inside the main doors of the apartment, I buzzed the number listed on the ad.

"Yeah," came a deep reply.

I swallowed hard. "Uh…we just talked on the phone about your ad."

Instead of responding like I had assumed the guy would, a buzz sounded, indicating that the door had been unlocked.

Taking a deep breath, I made my way to the floor and apartment listed on the piece of paper in my hand. Once I stood outside the door, I took another breath and knocked.

It opened, revealing…

"Rowan?" My eyes widened, not expecting to find him standing there.

"I thought that was you on the phone." He stepped to the side, swinging out his arm. "Come in."

I entered the apartment and turned as he shut the door. "You're looking for a roommate?"

He clicked the locks into place and came toward me. "Shit. That's an old ad."

My stomach fell. "Oh…okay. Well, I'll go then."

"Wait. You're looking to move?" he asked, grabbing the ad from my hand.

"Yeah," I said, running my fingers through my hair. "It's weird being at the apartment now that my brother no longer lives there. And there's too many…memories."

"I get that." Rowan started walking down the hall. "Did you want a tour then?"

"What?" I rushed to keep up with him. "I thought the ad was old?"

"It is but I kept getting a bunch of odd people wanting to move in with me, so I ended up taking the ads down. I obviously missed one."

"Oh." I shoved my hands in my pockets. "If you're still looking for a roommate, I would be down for that." *Smooth, Aiden. Real smooth.*

Rowan chuckled. "As long as you're not a crazy stalker, or someone who claims you're pregnant with my baby, or even someone who wants to use me to get close to my dad, you're free to move in anytime."

"That actually happened?" I asked, following him into an open area. To the right was the kitchen. Straight ahead were the patio doors that led to the balcony. A hall sat to the left and I could only assume the bedrooms and bathroom were that way. The apartment was a decent size. It was bigger than the one I currently lived in, so I definitely couldn't complain about the extra space I would have.

But what I noticed most was Rowan. Seeing him in broad daylight instead of the dim lighting of the bar, made me look at him harder. Dark scruff had grown in on his strong jaw. He wore a black T-shirt that hugged his wide frame along with ripped blue jeans that showcased thick thighs. Being there with him where it was just the two of us, sent my heart fluttering.

"Yeah, it did." Rowan went to the fridge and pulled out two bottles of water.

I stared after him, having to think for a second what he was referring to.

He handed me a bottle and leaned against the counter. "The first two I can expect but when women want to use me to get to know my father, I draw the line there. It's strange and they obviously have never met my mom. She's small but feisty as fuck."

I laughed, sitting at a stool at the island in the middle of the kitchen. "Sounds like my mom. But I can't say that I've ever had anyone want to use me to get close to my dad." The thought of that was weird to say the least.

"You're lucky." Rowan drank from his water, his eyes locking with mine.

I shifted in my seat, picking at the label on the plastic bottle. "If you aren't actually looking for a roommate anymore, I can find somewhere else to live."

"Nah." Rowan threw his empty bottle in the recycling bin. "I could always use the company anyway."

"Are you sure? I don't want you to let me move in just because…" My voice trailed off as his face morphed into a scowl.

"Listen, Aiden. I like you and have been thinking about you since we had a drink and nachos together. I regretted not asking for your number but now that you're here, it's like fate brought us together. I'm not suggesting anything else but I know that you need a friend, and so do I." He reached across the island and held out his hand. "So, I'm inviting you to move in if you wish."

"Yes," I whispered, returning the handshake.

"Welcome to your new humble abode, roomie." He came around to my side of the island and stopped a few feet away. "Come, let me give you a proper tour and then we can go from there."

FOUR

AIDEN

IT WAS MOVING DAY and I was trying not to show my excitement or nerves. I had never lived with anyone else outside of the military, my brother, or parents. I felt it was a step in the right direction, but some people didn't seem to agree.

"You're moving in with someone?" Tana Yates asked, grabbing herself a cup of coffee.

"I am. That's good, is it not?" I wasn't sure why I was seeking validation. Especially from her. But maybe it was because she was my sponsor, at the moment anyway, and I felt I had to get her approval. I wasn't sure. Maybe I needed a new sponsor. Not someone who looked at me a little longer than she should. It bordered on inappropriate at best, but I was new to this and didn't know exactly what the rules were. It wasn't like they made a handbook on this sort of thing.

"I don't know. You just joined AA a couple months ago and only come to one meeting a week…I just…" She chewed her bottom lip.

"I've been attending AA longer than a couple of months." It was court ordered. I just never told anyone that. *"I only transferred to this one recently, when my first sponsor moved away,"* I corrected her, not really appreciating the judgement rolling off of her.

"Well…" She huffed. *"Just be careful."*

"I'm here. This is me being careful, Tana." I spun on my heel and walked away but not before I caught the hurt written all over her face. I wasn't sure why. It wasn't like what I said was mean or anything. I just needed support. Was that too much to ask for?

"What the fuck do you have in this box, man?" Ashton, my twin brother, grunted as he carried a box of books into my new bedroom.

"Books," I told him.

"Books?" He set it down on my bed. "Since when do you read?"

"Since I can't drink anymore to take the edge off," I mumbled. It wasn't like I was having sex either, so reading would have to do. For now.

He stood, his eyes snapping to mine.

"Sorry." Shame rested on my shoulders. It wasn't his fault. None of this was his fault. It was mine and only mine.

"Don't be." He came up to me and pulled me into his arms.

I sighed, returning the embrace.

He cupped my nape, holding me at arm's length. "You good?"

"I am." Or I would be. Hopefully. One couldn't predict the outcome when it came to something like this.

"Good." Ashton released me and turned. "I think that was the last of it."

"Thank you for your help."

"Of course." He clapped my shoulder and went to leave my room when Rowan appeared in the doorway.

My stomach did a flip at the sight of him. It wasn't a new feeling when it came to someone from the same sex. I just hadn't been interested in someone for so long, I thought maybe something was broken inside of me. But it was like Rowan reached inside of me and unleashed something dark, something powerful. Something *sinister*. I wasn't overly dominant and would rather submit, but I hadn't trusted anyone enough to embrace that side of me. With Rowan, I imagined myself on my knees, staring up into his eyes and waiting for his instructions.

"All moved in?" Rowan asked me, his dark eyes searing into me.

"I am." I cleared my throat and pointed to my brother. "Rowan, this is my brother Ashton. Ashton, this is Rowan, my roommate, which I'm sure you already figured out."

"I figured as much." Ashton stuck out his hand. "It's nice to meet you."

"It's nice to meet you too," Rowan said, returning the handshake. "I'll let you get settled. If you need me, just call or text. My store is only a block away."

I thanked him and watched him leave. Once Ashton and I were alone again, I went to walk past him to start putting some things away when his cough stopped me.

"What?" I asked him, not really ready for an inquisition.

"So, you met him at a bar?"

"Yeah, and then we had nachos." I explained as well about the misunderstanding with the roommate ad that should have been taken down but wasn't.

"It's fate." Ashton sat on the edge of my bed. "You sure you're good?"

I sighed, turning to him. "What are you really asking me?"

"I just…I love you, Aiden, and I worry about you. Mom and Dad worry—"

"I know and I appreciate that. But I haven't had a drop of alcohol since the accident, if that's what you're really wanting to know." The words tasted bitter on my tongue. Maybe one day I would get used to saying them but for now, I wasn't.

"Alright." Ashton came toward me and pulled me in for another hug. "I love you."

"I love you too." I squeezed him back.

"Is Rowan good to you?"

My neck heated at the mention of his name. "Uh…I guess. We haven't known each other for long."

"Well…if he fucks up or hurts you in any way, let me know."

I leaned back, staring at my brother. My best friend. The other part of me I didn't deserve. "What are you getting at?"

Ashton lightly tapped my cheek. "Just saying that I don't give a shit what or who you're into as long as they don't fuck you over. That's all."

"I'm not into anything at the moment," I mumbled, running a hand through my hair. The room was filled with boxes, and I didn't even know where to start when it came to unpacking them.

"I'm going to head home. Unless you need help unpacking."

"No, thank you. You go and tell your Mrs. that I said hi and that she needs to teach me how to play poker."

"Will do." He chuckled.

Ashton gave me a third hug before leaving the room, the apartment door shutting a moment later.

Spending the rest of the day unpacking, I still couldn't believe that I had moved out of my old place and into Rowan's so quickly. I did have to pay a penalty because I had moved out before the lease was up on the old place, but I didn't care. It was worth it to get out.

Later that night, I sent the family group chat I shared with Ashton, our parents, and now Ashton's wife, Tabby, a text, letting everyone know that I was moved in. Dad had offered to help and while I appreciated the offer, most of the big stuff had been moved by delivery drivers after I ordered a brand-new bedroom suite. Ashton and I just moved the small things. I didn't have a lot of stuff. Nothing that I really wanted to keep anyway. Anything of sentimental value was still at our parents' house in my childhood bedroom. Even though we hadn't lived at home in years, our mom insisted on keeping our bedrooms the way they were. So, whenever we needed to come home, we had a safe space. I had a feeling that her sentiment was more geared toward me than Ashton, but we never commented on it.

I had just finished unpacking when the door to the room slowly opened. I turned, finding Rowan standing there. His big body filled the doorframe, his eyes moving around the room.

"You all settled?" he asked, his gaze finally connecting with mine.

"I think so." Truth was, I wasn't sure if I would ever get settled no matter where I was.

"Good. I'll leave you be then." He left the room before I could say anything. I didn't know what I could say in the first place.

Stay with me. Talk to me. Be with me.

Shoving those random thoughts aside, I finished putting things away. It was pushing just after midnight and, while I was tired and sore from the move, I didn't want to go to bed. That was when the noise happened. The voices taunting me, blaming me, accusing me of surviving when others didn't. Survivor's guilt was shit.

Taking a quick shower, I tried distracting myself from the nightmares in my mind and focused on the hot water raining down over my body instead.

When I was done, I stood in front of the mirror with a towel around my waist. Swiping my palm across the mirror, my eyes landed on the scars adorning my torso. I looked down at myself, running my finger along a pink jagged scar sitting on my hip.

"Please stop. Leave her alone. Take me." But even though those words left my lips, they chose not to listen. English wasn't their first language and they played it off that they couldn't understand me, but I knew they could. They just chose to ignore me.

Screams sounded in my ears.

Please let her die. It would be the best thing for her.

The memory slammed into me, knocking the breath out of my lungs and forcing me to my knees.

"Fuck." I squeezed my eyes shut, shaking my head back and forth, trying to ward off the evil and depravity of that moment that felt like a lifetime ago.

Giving myself a shake, I took a deep breath and pushed to my feet. I was in a fog as I dried myself off and slipped into plaid pajama pants. Throwing on a white T-shirt, I left the bathroom and took a step toward my bedroom, but something caught my attention.

Looking down the hall toward Rowan's room, I saw the light peaking from under the door.

My feet led me to his room and, before I knew what I was doing, I knocked.

"Come in," he called out.

Slowly pushing open the door, I cleared my throat. I didn't know why I was there.

Rowan was sitting on his bed with a laptop on his lap. "Hey, what's up?"

"I…" I blew out a slow breath, unsure how to ask if I could join him. Would it be weird that I didn't want to be alone and preferred to spend time with him instead? I wasn't sure what he was into exactly, but he had to have felt this unexpected connection between us.

Rowan sat up straighter, placing the laptop on the bed in front of him. "You okay?"

I shook my head.

"Come here." He patted the spot beside him.

Closing the door behind me, I made my way to the bed but stopped when I stood a foot away. "Is this weird? I mean…I just moved in, and we haven't known each other for long."

"It's only weird if you make it weird." He closed the lid to his laptop and placed it on his nightstand. "Sit, Aiden."

I sat, my body complying before my brain could catch up.

"What's going on?" he asked gently.

Lifting my knee onto the mattress beneath me, I turned to him. "I haven't slept in my own bed in months," I confessed. "I would rent a room at a motel and stay there instead."

"How come?"

I shrugged but thought over an answer. "I guess I didn't want to be alone. But then another part did want to be alone, just not in my own bed. It doesn't make sense but that's the truth. I even bought a new bedroom suite for here, but I don't…I just…"

"You don't have to be alone. Not anymore." Rowan sat back, leaning against the headboard and patting the spot beside him. "Come here."

I did as I was told and moved to the spot beside him, stretching out my legs in front of me. I wasn't sure where to put my hands, so I folded them on my lap and just breathed.

"Better?"

"I think so." I leaned my head back against the headboard and looked at him. He was wearing gray sweatpants and a black T-shirt. His light brown hair was messy on top of his head, like he had been running his fingers through them. Scruff had grown in some on his jaw as well and it made me wonder if something wasn't wrong. "You good?"

Rowan's head whipped around. "You're asking me if *I'm* good when you're the one who appeared to be on the verge of freaking out just a second ago?"

I shrugged.

He mirrored my pose, giving me a small smile. "Yeah, I'm good." His eyes dropped to my mouth, something flashing behind them.

My stomach did a flip. "Rowan."

"Yeah." He met my gaze once again. "I know."

"You do?" I frowned. "You don't know what I was going to say." Hell, I didn't even know what I was going to say.

"Nope." He crossed his arms under his broad chest. "I don't. Not exactly anyway. But I have a feeling that you're confused. You don't have to tell me about what. Just know that I'm here. I'll explain anything I can and help you in any way that I can as well."

I sat forward, crossing my legs under me. "Why? You don't know me, Rowan." I didn't even know myself.

"Sometimes it takes a little longer to know ourselves. Truly know ourselves."

I looked away, not realizing I had said that last part out loud. "I don't know what I want. I guess I just need a friend for right now."

"I can be that friend, Aiden."

I appreciated his words but there weren't a lot of people I trusted. Ashton was one but even he didn't truly know me. I wasn't sure how to let my guard down and just be myself when I didn't know who that person was.

"Why?" I whispered.

"Why not?"

"You don't want me." I looked at the closed door, a part of me wanting to run but then the other part, the most important part, wanted to stay. The part that just wanted to be held and cared for. The part that wanted to feel…safe. By myself and also with someone else.

"Listen." Rowan covered my hand that was resting on the bed between us. "You're safe here. With me. Within these walls. I know we hardly know each other but I would like to become friends. I'm not looking for anything more than that."

I blew out a slow breath. "I'd like to become friends too."

"Good." Rowan gave my hand a squeeze. "Do you like *The Office?*"

FIVE

ROWAN

IT WAS ON THE tip of my tongue to ask Aiden what exactly he was into, but I hesitated. The attraction was there, and I would bet my business on the fact he noticed it as well, but I didn't know him. I knew his name and that he was struggling with something but that was about it. So, I never pressed for more.

There was definitely something going on between us though. Maybe I was just overlooking things. Maybe I wanted that companionship so damn bad, my brain was conjuring things up that weren't actually true.

We got through half of the first season of *The Office* before he started yawning.

"Lay down," I blurted. Fuck, he was going to think I was a damn creeper but much to my surprise, he did as I suggested and curled onto his side. His eyes were still open, fixated on the TV sitting on my dresser.

"Thank you, Rowan," I heard Aiden mutter.

"For what?"

"For this." He sighed heavily, his eyes fluttering closed.

Reaching out, I brushed his bangs off his forehead. "You're welcome."

It was within that moment that I could see some of the tension leaving his body. I didn't know much about him. He had a brother and loving parents. But there was a dark part to him. A part I had seen time and time again in people closest to me. I prayed that he didn't have as shitty of a childhood as my parents had. They never told us all of the details, but I knew people. And I knew people who knew my father. People talked. While I didn't believe some of what they had said, I was sure some of the rumors had a bit of truth to them. It wasn't like I could ask my parents about it though, and there was no way I would ever bring it up to my dad and ask what was real or not. It also wasn't my business.

My phone took that moment to vibrate, bouncing on the nightstand beside me. A sour taste filled my throat, knowing that if anyone was trying to contact me at this time, it wasn't a good thing.

"You need to get out of this line of work, Rowan," my sister, Ettie, chastised.

I scoffed. "I have no idea what you're talking about."

"Seriously?" She glared at me and placed her hands on her hips. "You do realize where we're standing right? We're in a secret room in the basement under your damn store. I'm not stupid. And Mom and Daddy aren't stupid either. We worry about you."

"I'm a big boy." I stepped out from behind my desk and went up to her. She was older than I was but took after our mom, so she was tiny. But she sure as hell had a temper on her. There had been times where I wasn't sure how her husband put up with her fiery personality, but at the same time I understood. He looked at her like she was the only thing that mattered in his world. Along with their children, his life was complete.

"Doesn't matter if you're a big boy or not, if something happened to you…" Her chin wobbled.

"Hey." I pulled her into my arms, wrapping myself around her. *"I'm fine."*

She sighed, returning the embrace. *"You better be."*

And I had been. It would take awhile but I was cutting off all contact with several people. It just took time. If I up and quit right away, I would be searched out or worse, my family would. I didn't need that shit and would do what I could to prevent anything bad from happening. Starting with the person trying to get a hold of me currently.

Checking my phone, I frowned when I saw a text come in from an unknown number. They asked if I could meet up but anyone who knew me, knew they shouldn't be asking that through text.

I went to respond when Aiden shifted beside me.

He began mumbling words I couldn't understand but they reached a part of me that had never been reached. Something was wrong. Was he dreaming? Having a nightmare?

"Please stop," he suddenly said.

My eyes widened, my stomach sinking at the pleading in his deep voice.

"Leave her alone," he whimpered. "Take me instead."

"Shit." I touched his shoulder. "Aiden, wake up. You're having a nightmare."

He jumped and much to my surprise, threw himself into my arms.

My body was stiff and rigid, not expecting him to need me this way. No. He didn't need me technically. He obviously just needed to be consoled.

I wrapped my arms around him, held him tight, and ran my hand in circles along his upper back. His shirt was stuck to his sweat-soaked skin, his muscles bunching beneath the fabric.

He pushed his face into the crook of my neck, his body shuddering against me.

A part of me was tempted to place him back on the bed beside me but then another part, the part that needed this physical contact, held him even closer.

I leaned back against the headboard, trying to get comfortable.

Aiden let out a heavy sigh, resting all of his weight on me. He was heavy but the pressure from the position he was in eased some of the anxiety that had been sitting on my shoulders for a while now.

With some maneuvering, I was able to grab the comforter and pull it up over us.

Soft lips suddenly brushed along the side of my neck.

My body stiffened, my cock twitching between us.

Aiden's soft snores filled my ears, his hot breath fanning over my throat.

When he shifted on top of me, the movement rubbed against my crotch. I had to bite back a moan at the contact. He really needed to stop moving.

"Rowan," he whispered.

My eyes widened.

He sighed again, finally settling into a deep sleep.

"I got you," I told him softly, wishing there was something more I could do for him but for now, I would do what I could, and thought was right.

SIX

AIDEN

WHEN I WOKE THE following morning, I was met by the sun streaming in from the window. It felt warm on my face and lifted some of the dead, bitter weight that had been resting on my shoulders ever since I was forced to leave the Navy.

Something else was warm but it was beneath me instead. It was hard but comforting.

I didn't want to get up just yet, so I tightened my grip on whatever I was lying on. Letting out a sigh, I shifted, something bumping my crotch. It sent a tingle through my balls. My mind was suddenly filled with dirty images of me and a dark, mysterious stranger. I couldn't make out who it was, but I knew that it was a man. The silhouette of him enveloped me in a blanket of bliss.

Hands massaged. Mouths touched. Fingers kneaded.

A low moan rumbled from somewhere deep in my chest.

Someone coughed, the sound distant and breaking the spell of my delicious fantasy.

Lifting my head, I rubbed my eyes and looked around me. I frowned, noticing how I wasn't in my room. Memories came rushing back. It had been my first night living with Rowan as his roommate, but this room didn't look like the one I had moved into.

A throat clearing pulled my head around and I was met by heated eyes. They were a deep sapphire but so damn dark at the moment, they looked almost black. Why did I never notice that before?

"How did you sleep?" Rowan asked, his voice rough. "After your nightmare I mean."

I looked around me and was made very aware of how I was lying. I was on top of him, and I was hard. *Shit.*

Did I like it? Yes.

Should I like it? I wasn't sure.

Did it mean something more? Who the hell knew anymore.

Did I even want more? Yes. Damn straight I did.

But I pulled away from him like his touch burned me anyway. "I…this…this… shouldn't have happened. I'm sorry. I wasn't thinking."

"Aiden." He reached out for me.

I backed up and slid off the bed. My muscles ached like they always did after a night of restless sleep. "I can't do this."

"We didn't do anything. You came in here looking upset. I told you to join me. You fell asleep and you ended up having a nightmare. I held you while you slept. You were dreaming again this morning but from what I gather, it was a happier dream."

My cheeks burned at being caught having a dream that was most likely about him.

Rowan tilted his head, his dark eyes slowly sliding down the length of me. "Nothing happened."

I shook my head, dropping my hands to my crotch and shielding what I could only imagine was evidence of that dream. When my body hit the wall behind me, I jumped.

Rowan left the bed and tentatively came toward me. "Do you think I would take advantage of you like that? I realize we hardly know each other but I'm not that type of person. I promise, Aiden. Whatever you're going through, you're safe. You are safe. With me."

Lifting my hands, I tried warding him off, but he only came closer.

Once he was a foot away, his eyes moved across my face, searching for something. He was probably looking for answers to questions he never asked.

"What's going on?" he asked gently.

"I'm scared and confused. I feel like I've been backed into a corner, and I can't get out. I'm stuck and I don't like it," I confessed all in one breath. When the words left my lips, I wished I could take them back. There was no going back now, so I might as well own up to them.

Rowan sighed, running a hand through his short brown hair. "We all have nightmares but yours are more than that. They're memories, aren't they?"

I nodded, rubbing the back of my neck, trying to ease the tension that had rested on my shoulders for awhile now.

Placing my hands on my knees, I bent at the waist and took deep breaths.

The urge to leave this apartment, came on strong. Maybe somewhere new would be good for me. Maybe it would prevent me from wanting a damn drink. I looked around the room, searching for something but I wasn't sure exactly what I was looking for.

"Aiden?"

My skin tingled over my muscles and bones. Quickly leaving Rowan's bedroom, I went to mine with him hot on my heels.

"Aiden," he repeated, following me.

Ignoring him, I started rummaging through my bags. I slammed drawers open and closed. It had to be here somewhere. I couldn't have drank it all. Not yet. I always saved a bottle for emergencies.

"Aiden," Rowan barked, cupping my shoulder.

I shrugged him off but when he placed a hand on my shoulder again, I spun on him. He was a couple of inches taller than I was and he was bigger than me. The sudden move surprised us both, forcing him to stumble back a step.

"I need a drink," I heard myself say. My voice sounded far away. It seemed foreign to me in a way. I had been doing well. Or well enough. But I now suddenly needed something, anything, to take the edge off. Sex was few and far between for me and there had been no one I was even remotely interested in. Not until Rowan. But I wasn't sure if he swung that way. Hell, I wasn't sure if *I* swung that way. So, alcohol would have to do.

"No, you don't need a drink," I heard Rowan say. "It's not even eight in the morning."

"What the fuck do you know?" I mumbled, stomping around my room.

Before I knew what was happening, he crashed into me and wrapped his big body around me.

I struggled against him, not needing this at the moment. "Let me go."

But his hold on me only tightened.

"Rowan." I tried pushing him away, but the fucker was too damn strong. "Stop." My chest constricted, a lump suddenly filling my throat. My eyes burned, the rage inside of me growing. "Please…I can't."

"We just met but I feel like I've known you for a lifetime." His whispered truths slid over me. "It doesn't make sense. I know that it doesn't." His fingers ran through the hair at the back of my head. "But I'm here."

"I don't know you well enough for you to be here." But although I said the words, my arms still wrapped around him. My body still melted into him. And that rage, simmered.

"I don't give a shit about that," he murmured. "Everyone needs someone to be there for them."

"I have my brother," I said, my voice cracking.

"And I have my sister." Rowan tightened his hold on me. "But they have people of their own. Let me be yours."

A sob broke free, all of these emotions hitting me. They weighed me down, knocking the breath out of me to the point I couldn't control the cries of anguish leaving me. "It shouldn't have happened. It should have been me. I need a drink. I need them. *Fuck*."

Rowan didn't say anything as I rambled incoherent nonsense between my cries. Even though what I was saying didn't make sense, I felt almost…better in a way. I was still on the cusp of losing my mind and I needed that drink, maybe I always would, but now, I just felt stripped.

Raw.

It was like a layer had been ripped back, revealing some of my truth. It left me feeling vulnerable. If it were with anyone else, I would have been embarrassed. Because it was with Rowan, someone I hardly knew, maybe it seemed almost more manageable. He wasn't biased.

Rowan leaned back but his body remained close. He cupped the side of my neck. "How do you feel?"

"Exhausted," I whispered.

He gave me a small smile. "Can I ask you a question?"

I nodded. The guy had already seen me on the verge of losing it, so I really couldn't say no to him seeing any more of my fuckedupness.

"Do you have a drinking problem?" There was no judgement in his voice. No pity either.

My stomach twisted at the question. "So I've been told."

"You don't think you do?" he asked, tilting his head.

I shrugged. "I go to AA and I have a sponsor, but I think she's more interested in my dick than actually helping me through this shit."

Rowan's jaw clenched as he closed that final distance between us and pushed his pelvis into mine.

A shiver raced down my spine at the contact. My hand fell to his hip, pulling him closer. The contact calmed me in a way. It eased some of the anxiety scraping along my skin. Maybe he was right. Maybe he could be mine. If we just became friends, I could handle that. It would be nice having someone in my corner who didn't look at me and wonder when I would have my next relapse.

"Did you fuck her?" he asked, his question pulling me from my thoughts.

A laugh boomed through me.

His eyes widened a bit. "What's so damn funny?"

"Trust me, Rowan," I said once I calmed down. "I'm not interested in her or any woman for that matter."

He stared at me.

I realized what I said the longer time went on where he didn't say anything in response.

"You're not interested in—"

"Listen." I stood up taller and pulled him even closer. My dick twitched and I could feel his do the same. "I like this. I like you. But I'm fucked up. I have baggage. I do want to be your friend, but I don't know if I could ever be any more than that." I sighed. "And it's not because you're a guy," I quickly added. "Just want to make that part clear. I don't give a shit what you have between your legs or what you identify as. Just treat me well and I'm good." That was a truth I only just realized was in fact how I felt. It explained a lot. While sex could be enjoyable with the right person, I was more into just hanging out, talking and maybe even some cuddling. If sex happened, great. If not, that was fine too.

"Huh." Rowan placed his hands on my chest. "Looks like you're in luck, Aiden. Because I don't actually give a shit about any of that either. Just treat me well, like you said, and we're good."

I gave him a small smile. "Good."

"Very good," he murmured, glancing down at my mouth.

My heart sped up.

"Well." Rowan cleared his throat and backed away, a sudden cold draft washing over me. "I'll take you somewhere this afternoon or in a few days from now. Whenever you're ready." He went to the door and turned back to me. "I also meant what I said, Aiden. I'm good with being friends." Before I could comment, he left the doorway, the sound of a door shutting a moment later, forcing all the air in my lungs to leave me.

I wasn't expecting that. He didn't question me on not being interested in any woman, didn't even look at me like I had two damn heads either.

I almost wished he had. I almost wished he would have pressed for more. To find out what my desires were. What I actually liked and didn't like because fuck if I knew.

Getting ready for the day, it felt good to get at least some of my truths out there in the open. The weight of my baggage wasn't overly heavy at the moment, but I still wanted that drink. The sustenance as I felt the liquid burning its way down my throat until it settled in the pit of my stomach. Would it always feel like this? Would I be able to get over it or through it? Could I do this?

A part of me wished I was still in rehab, but I couldn't spend the rest of my life there. My therapist had told me that I was moving in the right direction, so I needed to take a chance and put myself out into the world.

I still worked at the center from time to time but the construction business I owned with my brother was where my true passion lay. Or so I was told. Apparently being good at your job meant that it was your life's calling to continue said work. I just wanted to not crave a damn drink anymore. Was that so much to ask?

Once I was showered, I went back to my room with a towel wrapped around my waist. I was holding clothes in my hands and just staring at them. Anxiety skated over my skin like tiny spiders. My throat suddenly parched. I took a deep breath and then another. I repeated it until I felt somewhat better. Or at least good enough to get dressed. I wasn't sure what sparked these anxiety-ridden moments. Anything could cause them. From making a coffee in the morning to catching the bus. I couldn't make sense of them or predict when they would happen. Anything was a possible trigger for me.

My phone chimed, indicating a text or maybe it was an email. I didn't know as I never set it up, but apparently people wanted me to have it so they could get a hold of me if they needed to. Ashton had set the phone up for me, but I never learned how to figure it out. I only answered phone calls or text messages from time to time but other than that, I stayed away from it.

Picking my phone up off my bed, I saw that a text had come in from Tana, telling me to call her.

I let out a harsh sigh, hit the call button, and waited for her to answer.

"Aiden, you missed a meeting," she said without even offering a single greeting.

"What?" I frowned. "No, I didn't. It's only Monday." I went to meetings on Wednesdays but was considering going on Fridays too.

"Yes, you did. You said you were going to start coming to the one in the afternoon which is held on Mondays," she explained.

"I never agreed to that. You're lucky you're getting me there on Wednesday nights." It didn't matter that the court ordered me to attend. She didn't need to know that.

"Listen, if you can't show up to a meeting, I don't know if I can continue being your sponsor."

"Tana, I never said I was coming to the afternoon meetings. I also don't think it works this way." But I couldn't be sure. I had tried Googling it but just the idea of going to these meetings and laying it all out for random strangers, almost caused a panic attack, so I stopped.

"Maybe I shouldn't be your sponsor anyway," she said, her voice softer now and hidden with something I wasn't sure I wanted to know.

"What are you talking about?" I placed the phone on speaker and set it on the bed so I could get dressed.

"I like you, Aiden, and I know it's unprof—"

"I'm going to stop you there." I couldn't believe what I was hearing. "I'm not interested."

She laughed. She actually fucking laughed.

I raised an eyebrow, glaring at my phone. "What the hell is so damn funny?"

"Come on, Aiden, I've seen the way you look at me."

"Getting mixed up with my sponsor…scratch that…*former* sponsor, is not healthy for me. I don't want a relationship. Not with you. Not with anyone." I wanted a friendship. A companionship. Maybe someone I could fuck around with a little. Even if I did in fact want a relationship, it wouldn't be with her.

I needed a dog.

Quickly slipping into my jeans, I left the zipper and button undone while I looked for a shirt to wear.

The door to my room suddenly opened, forcing me to spin around.

Rowan's eyes dropped to my waist, his nostrils flaring. When his gaze met mine, the dark orbs were now almost black.

I swallowed hard, my mouth going dry. I had never been on the receiving end of a look like the one he was giving me.

Tana was still talking about something, but I couldn't focus on her words as Rowan, standing in the doorway, sucked all the air from my lungs.

While she was going on and talking about how we would be good together, I couldn't help but watch him. He only raised an eyebrow, his gaze dropping to the phone sitting on my bed.

"Tana." I picked up the phone and turned off the speaker. "I have to go." I disconnected the call as Rowan took a step toward me.

"I need to know something," he said, his voice deep and rough. "I don't give a shit that you just moved in. I *need* to know."

Before I could ask him what he meant, his hand was around the back of my neck. He pulled me toward him, pressing his mouth against mine.

I stiffened at the unexpected contact. It had been so long since I had been kissed, truly kissed, that I wasn't sure what to do. Where should I put my hands? Should I kiss him back? I didn't care that he was a guy. I had never actually come out and say that I was bisexual. Is that how I identified? Maybe it had been so long, that I just wanted something. Anything really. Was I that desperate for attention?

"Relax," Rowan whispered against my lips.

My body did as he said. I melted into his touch, my eyes fluttering closed. Although the kiss was soft and gentle, it opened up things in me I had never felt before. I thought I was broken. I thought not knowing what I wanted when it came to sex wasn't normal. I was confused and not knowing what I wanted, added more to my drinking problem. It wasn't like I had been traumatized as a kid but there was something in me that wanted a relationship first before sex was even put on the table. Or I wanted to at least know the person for a few weeks before we fucked.

"Relax, Aiden," Rowan demanded again.

At that single command, something inside of me snapped. I cupped the back of his head, deepening the kiss and pushing my pelvis against his.

He jumped, a low growl leaving the back of his throat. In a quick move, he had me back against the wall.

I gasped, the movement giving him the only invitation he needed.

Shoving his tongue into my mouth, it pulled a moan from somewhere inside of me that had never been reached.

We may not have known each other for the few weeks like I originally thought I wanted but I connected to him on a level I had never experienced.

My cock twitched beneath my jeans, the fact that they were still undone, leaving little to the imagination.

Rowan nipped at my lips, sucking my tongue between his teeth. His hands gripped my hips before moving up my sides. The touch sent a shiver down my spine.

Much to my dismay, Rowan broke the kiss, licking along his swollen bottom lip. "I'm sorry."

"For what?" I asked, breathless.

"For kissing you like that." He leaned back but our waists were still pressed up against the other. His hand moved to the back of my neck and gripped it tight, his thumb brushing up and down along the spot just under my ear. "I just needed to see."

"See what?" I asked him, unable to pull my eyes away from his.

"If things could change." He cleared his throat and pulled away, his cheeks turning a light shade of pink. "I'll let you finish getting dressed."

"Wait." When he went to leave, I grabbed his arm. Linking my fingers in his, I closed the distance between us. "I've never done this before," I confessed. "But I knew when I first met you that there was something…even if it was little…there was something there. I like you and I want to see where this goes. Even if it's just a friendship or..."

"More," he added, his voice low.

"Yeah." I ran my thumb along the edge of his hand, holding it tight in mine and taking a step closer. I had no idea what I was doing but when our hands bumped my crotch and his breath caught, I knew that I wanted to do it with him.

No. I *needed* to do it with him.

"Well, I think we've already added more to that list, seeing as you slept in my bed last night."

A laugh left me, my cheeks heating as the memory of waking up on top of him came to mind.

"I'm sorry for freaking out earlier."

"You don't have to apologize. Not to me." Rowan circled his hand around my throat. "You hear me? You are safe. With me."

I nodded, a shuddered breath leaving me. "It's been almost six months since I've had a drink but every day, I worry that I'll have a relapse since I've had so many before. And I know that my parents worry. My brother worries. Everyone fucking worries. I also know that they mean well..." I looked up at him then. "But a part of me wonders if they expect me to fall off the wagon."

"Then prove them wrong, Aiden." He kissed me softly on the mouth. "Prove all of them wrong." He gave my hand a final squeeze, released me, and left my room.

Could I do what he said and prove everyone I knew wrong? Was that even possible? I didn't know but what I did know was that I meant what I told him. I did want to explore this thing between us.

I couldn't wait, although I was scared, to see where it took us.

SEVEN

ROWAN

I SHOULDN'T HAVE KISSED him. Not when we hardly knew each other but hearing Aiden talk to that woman, his apparent sponsor, and how she wanted to be with him, it unleashed this jealous beast in me. I had never been possessive over someone before. Especially not someone I hardly knew. The fact that he kissed me back after a little encouragement, unleashed a powerful force between us.

When his tongue had slipped into my mouth, it took everything I was made of not to ravage the fuck out of him.

I had spent years researching what I liked, and I found that I wanted to show Aiden that, with the right person, all forms of kink could be delicious.

I didn't want to force him into anything he wasn't comfortable doing but I had known all along something was there. It was small but I wanted to see if it could grow into something more. Something both of us needed.

Sending my sister a quick text, I made plans to meet up with her in a few days. I needed to talk to someone about this and she would either tell me I was crazy or to go for it with Aiden.

Shoving my phone in my pocket, my head lifted as Aiden came down the hall toward me.

He was wearing a black long-sleeved shirt with the sleeves pushed up to his elbows. His jeans were a dark blue with ripped knees, his blond hair was messy like he constantly ran his fingers through it, and a shadow of scruff covered his strong chiseled jaw. When our eyes locked, he only smiled and gave me a shrug.

My dick twitched, clearly liking the view.

The longer I stared at him, the more these new feelings rushed through me. They came on so fast, I couldn't pinpoint exactly what it was that I felt.

Aiden closed the distance between us, stepping up against the side of my body. His index finger curled around my pinky.

"What's wrong?" he asked, concern evident in the lines on his forehead.

"I'm pansexual and I've been with all sorts of people, but I've never been attracted to anyone like this and then you come along and everything I thought I knew, changes…well…everything," I said all in a rush.

His cheeks turned pink at my confession, and I found that I wanted to know what his ass looked like, if it was the same color.

"I lost my virginity back in high school because I felt I had to," Aiden said, pulling me from my thoughts of spanking him. He chuckled at a memory. "I wasn't into it, but I must have been a damn good actor, or she faked it. I guess I'll never know."

"I was sixteen, fucked some chick in my class. Wasn't into it. Fucked a guy I met at a party. Wasn't into that either. Tried a few more times over the years and again, nothing. I went to a random BDSM club and was approached by a transgender male. He still had a pussy because he wasn't sure if he was going to get the surgery or not. I realized at the time that I didn't care. I learned then that there is so much more to sexualities than just being straight, gay, or bisexual."

Aiden's eyes widened a bit, his mouth falling open.

"What did you do?" he asked, invested in my story.

"I fucked him in front of a room full of voyeurs. One of the hottest nights I've ever experienced." I shrugged like it was no big deal because it really wasn't.

"Oh…" Aiden coughed, clearing his throat. "What happened after that?"

"I thanked him because it made me realize what I was into. I learned to explore and that my desires are not so black and white. There's a lot of gray area in what I enjoy but no one has been lucky enough to explore that with me." Until Aiden, or so I hoped anyway.

"Do you still talk to him?" he asked, something flashing in his eyes.

I tilted my head, a slow smirk spreading on my face. "Why do you ask?"

"Just curious." He cleared his throat, waiting for my answer.

"I talk to him from time to time, but he's no longer single. He found someone and is finally happy, so if you're wondering if I still fuck him, the answer is no. I haven't been with someone in quite a while actually." I could almost see the relief leave Aiden. Looked like someone was jealous.

"I thought I was alone," Aiden whispered. "This whole time, I thought something was wrong with me because I couldn't figure out what I wanted. I'm still confused but I…"

"What?"

"I'm attracted to you, but this is fast, and I don't know what I want exactly or what I'm into or what I like but…" He linked his fingers in mine and lifted our joined hands. "I like this."

"I like this too." I winked, pulling away from him. "What are your plans for today?"

"Nothing really."

"Good." I sat on the couch and patted the spot beside me. "We're going to spend the day watching movies, eating junk food, and we may even cuddle a bit. If you're good at least."

Aiden joined me, sitting a little too far away for my liking but I wouldn't press. Not yet. But as the day went on, I hoped that he would end up back in my arms.

"So as long as I behave, you'll touch me?" A spark of mischief flashed behind his eyes.

"If you want me to touch you that is."

He leaned his head back against the couch. "There were times I didn't want to be touched." He looked at me then. "I thought something was wrong."

"Nothing is wrong with you," I said, a little too roughly.

He flinched.

"Sorry." I took a deep breath before blowing it out slowly. "There is nothing wrong with not wanting to be touched. Or not wanting sex. Or not wanting a partner. If you want to stay single for the rest of your life and raise a whole bunch of fucking plants, you can."

He chuckled.

"I'm serious."

Aiden sat forward, turning his body toward me. "Where have you been my whole life? I know that sounds cheesy, especially when we just met a few—"

"Stop right there." I shuffled closer, maybe a little too close if the sharp intake of breath that left him was any indication, but he was starting to piss me off. It wasn't his fault. But I didn't like these thoughts running rampant through him. "I'm going to say this again. I don't give a flying fuck if we met a second ago." I waved a finger between us. "I'm getting too damn old for games, Aiden. I like you. I liked waking up this morning with you on top of me. I liked that you came to my room last night because you didn't want to be alone. I liked that you *needed* me. *Me*. I'm damn near a stranger but you needed me." When he opened his mouth to comment, I caught his jaw. "I'd be very careful what you say next."

His pupils dilated.

"Is this fast? I don't know but who the fuck cares? My parents were attracted to each other when they first met. Hell, they didn't even know each other's names at that point either. My brother-in-law followed my sister to Italy. He had a mission and that was to get her to fall in love with him, even though he wasn't her type."

"My brother proposed to his girl the first night they met," Aiden told me.

"Then why the hell are you questioning this? Why do you keep saying this is too soon?"

"Because it's never happened to me." He shoved his hand out of my grip. "Things like this don't happen to people like me."

"What the hell you going on about? People like you. What does that even mean?" Was he a murderer? A bad person? I did my fair share of illegal shit but even *I* deserved a chance at happiness.

"It doesn't matter." Aiden stood from the couch and went to walk away but I caught his arm, pulling him back down beside me. "It does not matter," he repeated, his eyes filled with a pain I had seen one too many times in my father.

"But that's where you're wrong. It does matter." Before he could get away from me, I grabbed the back of his neck and crushed my mouth to his.

A low rumble slipped out between us. I wasn't sure who actually made the noise. Just when I thought the kiss would go a little further, Aiden shoved me back. His dark blue eyes were filled with fury.

"You can't kiss me and expect all of my shit to just disappear, Rowan." He stood and stomped down the hallway toward his room.

The sound of the door slamming closed, rippled through me.

It left me wondering what the hell had just happened and whose ass I was going to kick for leaving him so damn broken.

EIGHT

AIDEN

ROWAN AND I AVOIDED each other for the next week.

While that was the case, the tension between us grew.

Whenever I saw him, I went to say something but always thought better of it, so I kept my thoughts to myself. He only stared at me, waiting for me to say whatever it was that was on my mind, but I never did.

We fell into a quiet routine where we went our separate ways each morning. When we came home from work in the evening, I would go to my room. I didn't see much of him, and it pissed me off. I didn't want to live like this.

Rowan hadn't kissed me again since our fight, and I shoved him away. Not like he had a chance to anyway when we practically ignored each other.

But I couldn't get the few times I felt his lips on mine out of my head. They left me aching and throbbing. My dick hurt from having no contact. Blood pumped through me, leaving me a damn mess as each day went on where we didn't talk.

One night, I was pacing in my room. I was vibrating, ready to burst out of my damn skin. Running my hand back and forth through my hair, I ripped and pulled at the strands. I needed a release. Something to curb this itch. Something to take the edge off.

I needed a drink.

The door suddenly slammed open, revealing a red-faced Rowan.

"I'm sick of this shit. Not talking. Not even acknowledging each other. I might as well be living alone." He took a step toward me. "You wanna fight? We fight. You wanna yell and scream and burn the fucking world down, I'll do it right along with you. But this ends. Now. And before you say it again, yes, I know that we haven't known each other for long. I know that you've only been here for just over a week. Maybe longer. Maybe less. I can't fucking think straight so time is lost on me."

"Why?" It was a stupid question when I felt the same way. I hated not talking to him, but I was so fucked up and in my head, that I didn't know how to tell him how I felt or what exactly it was that I wanted because hell, even I didn't know.

"Why the hell do you think, Aiden? You can't deny this connection between us. You can't deny that you are hard as fuck right now and I'm losing my damn mind over you. Over this. Whatever this is between us. I don't care if we don't do anything more than just talk but we have to talk. This avoidance ends."

"You've been avoiding me too," I reminded him.

He sucked in a sharp breath, trying to take control of the situation. "Aiden, I'm fucking warning you."

"You don't know me, Rowan," I pointed out, taking a step toward him. "You don't know the shit I've been through. You want to talk? Why? So you can fix me?" I chuckled, but the humor was never there. "This doesn't even make sense. I shouldn't want you. Not like this. Not so fucking soon."

"Stop," he shouted, closed that final space between us, and pushed me. "Stop. Just fucking stop."

"I shouldn't have moved in here."

As soon as those words left my lips, he charged for me. I didn't have time to comprehend what was going on. When Rowan crashed into me, his big body shoved me up against the nearest hard surface. His mouth came down hard on mine, our teeth knocking together. He shoved his hands in my hair, forcing my lips apart with his tongue.

I ran my hands over his hard torso, needing to feel something, anything. I needed him to take me out of my head.

Rowan broke the kiss, leaned back, and pulled his T-shirt up and over his head.

I never had a chance to truly look at him before he was back on me.

Grabbing my jeans, he ripped open the fly, the button popping off at the rough movement.

Reaching around him, my hands roamed up his hard back. Once they reached his nape, I deepened the kiss and swallowed his moan.

In a quick move, Rowan broke the kiss and spun me around. Slipping his fingers beneath my shirt, he pulled the fabric up my torso. I took the hint and lifted it up and over my head.

He stepped closer, pushing his pelvis into the seat of my ass and shoving my arms up over my head. A hot mouth kissed my shoulder, his hips undulating against me.

"Rowan," I whispered.

"Shut the fuck up." He spun me back around so I was facing him. His eyes were wild as they searched my face. For a sign? For a hint that I wanted him to stop? "Tell me again how we hardly know each other. How it's too soon. Too fast. Too fucking confusing. Tell me."

I swallowed hard. "It's too fast. We had dinner together once and I'm now your roommate but this, whatever this is, it doesn't make sense."

"You sure about that?" he asked, his voice taking on a deadly tone.

"Yes." I lifted my chin. "I'm sure."

"Good boy." He spun me back around, pushing me face first into the wall. With his palm pressing against my cheek, he shoved his free hand into my jeans. When he wrapped his fingers around me, I jumped.

The shot of pleasure was almost too much to handle. I hadn't been touched in so long, not even by my own hand, I was sure I wouldn't last long no matter how hard I tried fighting it.

"You're going to come. Against your wall. Against this bag here on the floor." He kicked my backpack. "Against the side of the dresser. You're going to leave it and let it dry. I want you to see it. Every time you come into this room; you're going to see the evidence of what I can do to you. Of how I make you feel." Rowan pulled my cock out of my jeans, roughly stroking from base to tip. When his fingers pinched the head, a whimper escaped me. "You're going to be reminded every single fucking time you enter this room that this isn't fast. That this isn't confusing. That this isn't too damn soon. Everything happens for a reason, Aiden. And I'm going to prove it to you."

Rowan pressed his palm against my cheek. My dick, hard and throbbing, in his other hand. The faster he stroked, the higher the pleasure rose.

My chest rose and fell with ragged breaths, my heart beat erratically behind the walls of my rib cage. As much as I wanted to touch him, to see his face as his hand pumped my cock, I was frozen in place. I couldn't help but submit to him. It had been something I longed to do for years. Even before leaving the Navy, but a lot of the women I had been with wanted to be dominated themselves. I couldn't find that right person to give my control to. Not like I trusted a whole lot of people when it came to sex anyway.

Rowan pushed his pelvis against me, grinding into my ass. "Stop thinking, baby. It's just you and me here."

The feeling of his erection sent me over the edge.

A harsh groan left me, my eyes rolling into the back of my head. My release poured out of me in thick streams, landing on the wall and the items at my feet like he had wanted in the first place.

He pinched the tip of my dick, forcing a whimper from my lips. The slice of pain made my eyes roll to the back of my head. It hurt but felt so damn good at the same time. He didn't release me. He only kept pumping my dick even though I'd already had a release.

"Please. God." I shivered. "It's too sensitive."

"It's never too sensitive." His hand picked up speed, not letting me have a moment of reprieve. My dick grew, hardening once again at his touch.

"Good boy," he whispered, placing a soft peck on my cheek. He stuffed my hard cock back into my jeans and did them up for me. "Keep your hands against the wall, don't move and don't even fucking think about touching yourself."

Rowan moved to the chair I kept in the corner of the room. Even though he told me to stay put, I could still see him at least. When he sat, he pulled his long, thick cock out of his sweatpants.

My throat dried, watching him wrap his hand around the veiny shaft.

With his eyes locked on mine, he stroked, pulling at his own dick. He grunted, moving his hips in sync with his hand.

No words slid between us as he jerked himself off in front of me.

My mouth watered, itching for a taste. But before I could even fathom doing such a thing since I really didn't have much experience in that area, Rowan groaned, his release coating his hand.

A breath I didn't realize I had been holding, left me as I watched him put himself away.

He rose from the chair and came toward me. He wiped himself off on my stomach, my abs twitching at the soft touch.

"Do you have any plans for the rest of the day?" he asked, his voice low.

"No." *Just hanging out with you, I hope.*

"Good, I—" Suddenly, his phone dinged, forcing a frown on his handsome face. He pulled his cell from his pocket, a soft curse leaving him.

"Everything okay?" I asked, turning toward him.

"It will be." Rowan sighed. "It has to be."

"What's going on?" It wasn't any of my business, but I needed him to know that I was there for him, much like he insisted that he was there for me.

"My line of work hasn't always been legal and I'm trying to change that. But some people aren't overly happy about that either. I'm also learning that some individuals don't know how to take no for an answer." He shoved his phone back in his pocket. "It doesn't matter. They can wait." He grabbed my hand and headed for the door, pulling me along with him. "Right now, I'm going to spend time with you and convince you that this is right."

NINE

ROWAN

STROKING MY DICK IN front of Aiden had been the hottest thing I had ever done. I wasn't sure if was because it was him or because we somehow had this unexpected connection, but I had never come so damn hard by my own touch.

Add to the fact that he listened to me when I told him to keep his hands against the wall, it forced this newfound awareness deep inside of me. Especially when he was once again hard and I wouldn't let him do anything about it.

While we watched a movie, I couldn't help but notice how right this was. Sitting there in silence with him. His body beside me, our thighs touching, his hand in mine, it just felt...normal.

He often shifted beside me, struggling with whatever internal thoughts he was having. It made my chest tighten, knowing that there wasn't much I could do to help him. Especially when I had my own shit to deal with as well.

My mind traveled back to that text.

Call me.

Two words that didn't mean much to most but they sure as hell meant something to me.

"What's wrong?"

My head whipped around.

Aiden was staring at me, a deep frown between his brows.

"You think something's wrong?" How the hell could he know me so well already?

"I do but I'm only making assumptions. You have been chewing on your thumb for the past hour though, so I'm thinking I'm right."

"I'm good," I told him because what could I really say? Sure, I was attracted to him, but he had been right in saying that we didn't really know each other. So, I very well couldn't tell him that I had spent years helping people find out shit, most of said shit being illegal. And I couldn't tell him that I used to sell my body for sex and that my one and only client fell in love with me and became stalkerish. Add to the fact that this guy could have made me fall in love with him just the same, leaving him had hurt. It still hurt and I didn't know how to deal with it.

Aiden chuckled, shaking his head. "Right and I'm not an alcoholic."

My jaw clenched. "I am good, and it would be best for you if you didn't question me." It didn't matter that Aiden was right. He needed to learn not to press but I also needed to learn not to be an asshole about it.

His smile fell, his pupils dilating.

I smirked, turning my body toward him. "That's interesting to me."

"What?" he whispered.

"Your pupils dilate when I tell you to do something or…" I leaned closer, our mouths mere inches apart. "When I threaten you."

His breath caught. "I…I'm not overly dominant. Never have been."

Shifting closer to him, I threw my leg over his lap, holding him in place. A nice shade of pink hit his cheeks, his cock jumping beneath my leg.

"Even if you were dominant, Aiden, it wouldn't matter because I'd still overpower you." He shifted beneath me. I liked feeling the struggle within him.

"That's what I need." He pulled his hand from mine and rested his arm across my lap. "I think."

"You don't have to figure out what you need right now, Aiden." I cupped his cheek, sliding my hand down to his throat. "We can figure that out later. But until then, we can learn what you want. The rest can come over time."

His Adam's apple bobbed behind my palm.

"Okay?" My eyes dropped to his mouth, needing to taste him but at the same time, not wanting to spook him either.

"Okay but…" He leaned his head back against the couch. "Just please don't hurt me."

"Never, baby." I turned his head toward me and placed a soft peck on his lips, needing that connection with him.

"Thank you for earlier," he murmured against my mouth.

"It was hot as fuck." I nipped his bottom lip, making him jump.

"It was." He leaned back, licking along the spot I bit. "I've never experienced something like that before."

"I've done a lot of shit over the years but that moment with you, was by far the best." I winked, shifting closer but I knew that no matter how close we were, it would never be enough.

A slow grin spread on his face and for the first time since I had known him, that smile actually reached his eyes.

"This feels—"

"If you say that this feels fast one more time, I'll bend you over right here and make you wish you never moved in with me."

"Fuck," he whispered, shaking his head. "No. I was going to say that this feels safe. Jesus, Rowan. Leave a little to the imagination, will you?"

"Fuck that noise." I cupped his jaw, digging my fingers into his cheeks. "I like you. I liked those little noises you made when I made you come. But I especially liked having your eyes on me when I stroked my cock for you."

"I liked watching you," he confessed, his eyes never straying from mine.

"Oh, I know you did and we're going to explore that eventually." Fucking him in front of a room full of people was now a goal. Or maybe fucking someone else while he was tied up and couldn't do anything but watch. Either way, we were going to play.

"I'm down for anything." Aiden pushed my leg off of him and stood from the couch. He went to the kitchen and came back a moment later with two bottles of water in hand.

"Are you really down for anything?" I asked, leaning against the other side of the couch and stretching out my legs in front of me.

"I haven't done a whole lot." Much to my surprise, he straddled my waist. "But for whatever reason, I feel comfortable with you. When I realized that it was you who lives here, I was thankful because I was pissed at myself that I never got your number after we shared nachos."

"I know." I placed my hands on his hips, liking this moment with him. "I even tried searching for you on every social media outlet I could think of but when I only had your first name, it was a little hard." I could have utilized my skills and searched him out another way but that was too damn stalkerish.

Even for me.

"You did?" Aiden raised an eyebrow.

"I did." I lifted his shirt, my cock twitching beneath his ass at seeing my dried cum on his stomach.

"That roommate ad was left up for a reason," he murmured, pulling his shirt up and over his head.

My mouth dried at the sight before me. He was hard in all the right places. I never noticed before, but it looked like he had gained some weight since I had first met him at that bar.

"Have you been to that bar since the night we met?" I asked him, needing to know every single thing that made him tick.

"Once." He grabbed the hem of my shirt, lifting it up my stomach. "I hoped that maybe you would just randomly show up but I haven't been back since. It hasn't been easy of course but I've been trying to avoid places that serve alcohol. There's usually a family thing that I go to once a month. It's a whole bunch of us. My parents. Their friends. But I haven't been going because I don't want them to not have alcohol just for me. And I feel…"

I sat up, pulling my shirt up and over my head. "How do you feel?"

Aiden glanced down at my naked torso. "I feel lost at times. Like I don't belong. Every time I go to these functions, I feel like they're expecting me to relapse. It's like they're waiting for it to happen." Sitting between my spread legs, he ran a hand through his hair. "I don't know. I'm sure they might not even think that but it's how I feel."

"It makes sense." I wrapped myself around him, running my hands down his strong back.

"I just want to feel normal," he whispered.

"How do you feel right now? With me?" I didn't want to push him into doing anything he wasn't ready for but if he told me to fuck him, I wouldn't say no. Until then, I wouldn't hint. Maybe fool around a little. Give each other a few orgasms. But the full deed would happen when he was truly ready.

"I feel…" His dark blue eyes searched my face. "Safe."

"You are safe, Aiden." I kissed the corner of his mouth. "I promise you're safe. Anything you need, I'll do my best to give it to you. And if I can't, we'll figure out somehow to make it happen. Even if it's not from me."

He leaned back. "What are you saying?"

"I'm saying that if we have sex and it's not enough for you, I'm fine if we include someone else." My stomach twisted at the thought, but I meant what I said. I would do anything to help him through his shit.

"I think us having sex would be enough for me but thank you. Most guys wouldn't want to share."

I grunted. "As long as I'm there, I don't give a shit who you fuck because I know it's me who gets your cock hard."

He chuckled. "Are you sure? Maybe I'm thinking of someone else."

"The fuck?" I shoved him, forcing him onto his back. "Want to say that again?"

His laughter deepened. "I think bringing someone else into this is a bad idea."

"You like pissing me off, don't you?" I growled, pushing my waist between his legs.

Aiden's eyes darkened. "Yes, I do actually."

I couldn't help but laugh at his honesty.

Placing my arms at either side of his head, I looked down at him. "I don't mind fucking in front of people or even just messing around in public. I'm willing to try anything once but you're probably right. I've had threesomes before but with you…" I scowled, shaking my head. "I don't think that'll ever happen," I told him, needing him to know that he could tell me his truths, his desires.

"I've never had sex in a room full of people. My brother was the adventurous one between us."

"We can change that." I grinned. "Trust me."

Aiden cupped the back of my neck, pulling me down to meet the hard impact of his mouth on mine. "I do," he whispered. "I do trust you."

I growled, slipping my tongue between his lips and forcing a moan to fall between us. The kiss deepened, our breathing picking up. My hips started undulating against him. We worked up a rhythm, sounds of pleasure leaving us both as we were grinding into the other.

"Fuck." I licked and sucked at his tongue, nipping his swollen lips.

Aiden reached around me, cupping my ass and lifting his hips with mine.

"You're so fucking hard, baby boy." I broke the kiss, trailing my tongue down the length of his jaw.

"So, are you," he panted, his eyes fluttering closed.

"For you, Aiden. I'm hard for you." I leaned down to his ear. "Imagine us in a dark room with people standing around us."

He moaned, his cock swelling against me.

"Imagine I'm inside of you. My big dick is filling your ass. It hurts but feels so good. You can't help but moan and whimper for me. You beg me for more, to go harder, faster. Everyone standing around us waits. Some of them are kissing, some are even fucking. You don't see it, but you hear them." I nipped his earlobe.

"Rowan," he groaned.

"You're so close," I told him. "You plead for me to let you come."

"Yes," he whined. "Please, baby. Let me come."

"Everyone wants you to come too," I whispered in his ear. "Let's give them what they want." I pulled away from him, moving down the length of his body. Ripping open his jeans, I kept my eyes on his as I pulled his jeans down his hips.

Aiden watched me the whole time, probably wondering what I was going to do.

I winked and lowered my mouth onto his swollen cock.

He groaned, lifting his hips.

I knew he wasn't going to last long but it didn't matter. I *needed* to taste him.

Wrapping my hand around his dick, I stroked it in time with my mouth. I pulled and tugged at him, needing his pleasure.

His chest rose and fell, his breathing picked up when my name suddenly left his lips on a harsh shout.

His release coated my tongue, the salty essence making my taste buds tingle.

Once he calmed down, I crawled up the length of his body. Sticking my finger in my mouth, I wiped the cum off my tongue and ran it along his lips.

His mouth parted, his nostrils flaring.

I winked, closed that distance between us, and let the remainder of his release slip from me to him.

He moaned, deepening the kiss.

"You like tasting yourself, Aiden?" I asked, lifting my head.

"Apparently so." He waggled his eyebrows.

I chuckled, placing a final kiss on his lips before sliding off of him.

Grabbing our shirts, I handed him his and placed mine back on.

"What are you doing?"

"Getting dressed." I looked at him. "Why?"

"But…" He glanced down at my lap. "What about you?"

"You will learn really quickly that I don't do something to get anything in return." I pinched his chin and kissed him hard. "I wanted to taste you and I did."

"So did I." He winked.

A laugh boomed through me. "Touché, baby boy."

"Thank you." Aiden put his shirt back on and righted his jeans. "I mean it."

"I know and you are welcome."

Silence fell between us, and I realized that while he had only just moved in the other day, I could easily see myself being in a relationship with him.

I just hoped that he could eventually see the same thing.

TEN

AIDEN

ROWAN REVEALED THINGS IN me I never knew were there before meeting him. His dominant personality called out to the submissive in me. I remembered back to a time where I wasn't so compliant. Before I was discharged from the Navy, I was more aggressive when it came to sex and what I liked, but that had only been because I couldn't find someone to overpower me. Casual hookups had gotten old real fast. So, I couldn't really venture out and find what I wanted and enjoyed before it was too late.

We had been living together for a few weeks already. Though we started messing around right away, we still hadn't had sex. I wondered if he was waiting for me to beg for it, but I hadn't yet, so he never hinted.

I liked what we were doing. Exploring the foreplay we shared between us was hotter than any of the sexual encounters I'd ever had.

I had never given a blowjob before meeting him and when I told him, he never seemed to care.

"You have a hot wet mouth, Aiden. If you make me come and I know you will, then you're doing it right."

I couldn't help but laugh since I still didn't know what I was doing. Insecurity settled in the pit of my stomach over not knowing how to please him when he had done so much for me already.

"I'll guide you."

There were times where Rowan would get a text, or a phone call and his mood would suddenly switch and take a turn for the worse. His anger over whoever was trying to get a hold of him, would come out in the way he was with me.

"Choke on my cock, Aiden."

"That's such a good boy."

"You suck dick so fucking well."

The vile things he said to me, the rough way he handled me, it was like he was trying to mask his frustration and take it out on me instead.

I never complained but I often wondered if it was an ex who was trying to get a hold of him.

One night, I was trying to sleep. Rowan's arm was thrown over my middle, his deep snores sounding in my ear.

After that first week where we hardly talked, he had insisted that I sleep in his bed. When I had joined him the first night I moved in with him, he told me it was the best sleep of his life. So ever since we stopped avoiding each other, we shared his bed.

His phone vibrated and I almost expected it to wake him up. He only stirred beside me, letting out a soft sigh.

I kissed his forehead, slipping out from under his arm and left the bed. After using the bathroom, I went to join him when I saw his phone going off. The screen kept lighting up. Who the hell was trying to get a hold of him at this time?

Walking around the bed, I picked up his phone to flip it over when a text caught my eye.

Unknown: Why the fuck are you ignoring me?

As soon as that text disappeared, another one came in.

Unknown: I need you, Rowan. We were so good together.

The texts came in one after another.

Unknown: Does your little toy know what you used to do for me?

I frowned, my heart jumping. Was this person talking about me? Unless Rowan had someone else he was messing around with. I wasn't sure. It wasn't like we ever really talked about being exclusive to each other.

Unknown: I hope you think of me when you fuck him.

This person was unreal.

Unknown: Tell Aiden I said hi.

He knew my name? How the hell could he know that?
"Aiden."
I jumped, finding Rowan sitting up in bed. "Who is this person?"
He grabbed the phone from me and placed it back on the nightstand. "I guess we need to talk."
"What the hell is going on? Why does this person know my name?"
Rowan turned on the lamp. "Because he's a hacker and knows how to find out shit." He patted the spot beside him. "Sit."
"This doesn't even make sense. How could he do that? That's not possible." Not that I knew much about hacking but there was no way someone could do that with so little information. Was there?

71

"Sit." Rowan patted the spot beside him again. "Please."

I slid onto the bed, moved to the spot beside him, and pulled the blanket up and over my lap. "Is this the same guy who's been trying to contact you these past few weeks?"

"Yeah." He took a breath. "My parents were hackers. They would find out information for people. When they retired, I took on that role because I get bored. I do own a store of antiques, books, anything really. But that's not what brings in the money."

"Who's this guy?"

"I met him on the dark web." He ran a hand through his dark hair. "He wanted an actual relationship, but I told him I just wanted some fun. He ended up asking me to send him videos of me jacking off. I didn't say no because if you haven't noticed, I like being watched."

My body heated as the memory of the first time we messed around slid into my mind. Watching him stroke himself had definitely been something I enjoyed and wanted to explore more of.

"So…he's been stalking you ever since?"

"Sort of." Rowan sighed. "It comes and goes but now that he knows about you, he'll probably try even harder to get in touch with me."

"How does he know my name?"

"I put you on the lease to my apartment. He could have hacked into the apartment manager's records. He could have seen you come and go from this place. There are so many ways he could have found that out. I also have your name and number in my phone."

"That makes sense, but I didn't even know that was a thing."

"Welcome to the darker side of technology, baby boy."

"Have you gone to the police?" It was a dumb question, especially since they didn't meet in the conventional way.

"No, I haven't. He's never been dangerous. It's more annoying than anything." He paused, searching my face. "I really like you. A lot. This feels right, Aiden." He grabbed my hand for added effect. "But I've done a lot of shitty things to make a quick buck. So, if you want to end this and move out, I get it. It'll hurt but I completely understand."

"No." I linked my fingers in his. "I like you too and besides, no one is perfect."

Rowan let out a deep breath, almost like he was relieved over my words. "Thank you."

"Is this something to worry about though?" I had never dealt with something like this. Even though I had been in the Navy, and we went through hell at times, literally, I had a team at my back. Never once have I ever had to deal with a psycho ex or a stalker in this case.

"It's fine." Rowan gave me a small smile for reassurance. "He's going to have to get over it."

"That doesn't make me feel better," I grumbled, moving to the spot beside him.

Slipping his hand under the blanket, Rowan cupped my inner thigh. "It's nothing to worry about."

"Rowan." I turned toward him, the movement making his hand fall from my thigh and brush against my dick. "I know people who may be able to help."

"Yeah, so do I." He finally looked at me then. "I don't want to involve my parents but if I need to, I will. It's just frustrating as fuck." He sighed, pulling a small laptop out of his nightstand.

"If you need some privacy to get some work done, I can leave." As soon as those words left my mouth, he grabbed onto my dick. The rough move made me jump, forcing a surprised grunt from my lips.

"I don't fucking think so." His head whipped around. "I know we've only been doing our thing for a few weeks, but you will learn very quickly that I'm possessive as fuck. And where I go, you go."

My dick twitched.

Rowan smirked.

I rolled my eyes. "Fine."

He chuckled, patted my now semi-hard length, and leaned back against the headboard. "I could use your help anyway."

"My help?" I shuffled closer. "What could I possibly help you with?"

"Moral support." A deep frown settled between his brows as he worked away on his laptop. I didn't know a whole lot about computers. Give me a rifle and I could take it apart, clean it, and put it back together before you could say semi-automatic. But a computer? I used them for games and social media. Maybe to check an email or two. Ever since my accident, I did my best to stay away from them to avoid any mention of alcohol.

While Rowan continued working, he would curse every so often, rub the spot between his eyebrows, and curse some more.

Although he would tense up every so often, I noticed how whenever I shifted and our thighs would touch, he would sigh. His body relaxed at the mere touch of mine.

"I'm going to have to head to my store," Rowan finally said a couple of hours later.

"Okay." I nodded toward his laptop. "Couldn't find anything?"

He closed his laptop, his jaw clenching. "I found enough."

My heart stuttered.

"I asked around. Others have heard of this fucker, and they said he's unstable. I didn't know. I was having some fun. I didn't expect the guy to fall in love with me."

My heart stuttered at that, a tremor of unease gripping me tight.

Rowan looked at me then, raising an eyebrow. "Problem?"

Clearing my throat, I shifted beside him. "No."

"Aiden." His eyes darkened. "Tell me."

"Hearing that he's in love with you makes me jealous." I lifted my chin in defiance. "Happy now?"

Rowan moved his laptop to the side. Pulling the blanket off of us, he wrapped his fingers around his cock. "You have nothing to be jealous over. This?" He pinched the crown of his thick length. "Is yours. You can suck it, stroke it, fucking nuzzle it…anything you want, it's yours to do with as you please."

"Rowan, I know that, I just don't…I have no idea. I wasn't expecting you to have a damn ex and…" I drew in a sharp breath. "Were you in love with him?"

"No, but I won't deny the fact that I could have fallen in love with him. He's a damn good liar. Made me believe things that weren't real. I cared for him. I still care for him but only because I don't want anything to happen to him. He's unwell and I only want him to get some help."

"I understand that, but maybe you were in love with him and just didn't know it. It's fine if you were," I offered. "I—"

"What the hell did I just say?" Rowan cupped the back of my neck. "Do I need to shove my cock down your throat to pacify you? Will that make you feel better and stop these irrational thoughts?"

My dick twitched at what he was suggesting.

"Answer me, Aiden." His grip on my neck tightened. "Tell me what you need."

"I need for you not to hurt me," I murmured. "That's it."

The hard lines on his face softened. He released me and leaned back against the headboard. "Put your head on my lap."

I laid down and did as I was told. His cock was at half-mast beneath my head. Somehow, feeling it twitch beneath me and knowing that I caused that reaction in him, eased some of the anxiety resting on my shoulders.

Rowan ran his fingers through my hair. "Better?"

"Yeah." I wrapped my arms around his waist.

"Good." He grabbed his laptop once again. "I'm going to work but if you need to calm down even more, you know what to do."

"I do." I never thought that giving him blowjobs could be relaxing. Babies had soothers, pacifiers, whatever you wanted to call them, to calm them down. How could sucking someone off do the same?

"A lot of people find it soothes them," Rowan answered.

My cheeks heated, not realizing I had spoken out loud. "It's actually a thing?"

"It is but we don't have to worry about that. We can just do what feels right for us. If it feels right for you to suck on my dick to help you sleep or to calm you down, then go ahead and do it. But if that's too weird for you, then we can try something different."

I rolled onto my back, staring up at him.

"This is new for you, so we'll just take it one day at a time." He ran his fingers down my cheek. "Okay?"

"Okay."

"Perfect." He gave me a small smile. "Now be a good boy and be quiet so I can work."

I chuckled, rolling back onto my side and snuggling my face into his crotch. The scent of him was all Rowan and spice, everything that made up him. Just being there, in his bed, with his fingers lazily running through my hair, was calming.

But I still couldn't help but wonder what his ex wanted and how far he would go to get what he was looking for.

ELEVEN

ROWAN

IT TOOK A WHILE for me to figure out exactly what I was into when it came to sex. I spent many years fucking anyone and everyone I could. Dated a few women, a few men, a couple at the same time. But it never satisfied me. Not emotionally. Hell, not even physically at times.

Before I met Aiden, I had gone without sex for a few months and decided to use my own hand instead. I knew what I liked and didn't like. I was willing to try anything at least once and as long as I had the trust of my partner, I was down for anything.

Meeting Aiden opened up something inside of me. Something I had no idea was even missing in the first place. Being with him, hanging out, talking, fucking around, it just felt right. It felt normal. I had been with guys before, but it had never felt like this.

As I got dressed, I couldn't help but glance at Aiden every so often. He was sitting on my bed, the blankets covering his lap while the rest of him was bare. He was playing on his phone. His dark blond hair was messy, a couple of days worth of scruff had grown in on his strong jaw, but he was perfect. He appeared to be relaxed. For the first time since I met him, he almost looked comfortable. I knew he was struggling. He would probably struggle for the rest of his life. But right now, in this moment, it was as if he knew he was safe.

I had to go to my store. I needed to figure out exactly what my ex, fling, whatever you wanted to refer to him as, wanted and why he wouldn't leave me alone.

Miguel Sincero came into my life at a time when I was lonely. But I never led him on. He knew right away that I just wanted to fuck around. That was it. I didn't want a relationship but even though I had told him so, we had become closer. Closer than I would have liked. He gave as good as he got and I used him. Guilt resonated on my shoulders that I wasn't firm enough when I told him it was over.

Regret settled deep in the pit of my gut, knowing his guy was someone who wouldn't back down and he clearly didn't like that I had ended things between us.

A sour taste filled my throat as the memory of the last text conversation between us slid to the forefront of my mind. He had asked me if I was in love with Aiden. It was way too damn soon for that, but Miguel didn't believe me when I told him no. If something happened to Aiden as a result of Miguel's jealousy, I would burn down the fucking world.

"I can feel you staring," Aiden said, not looking up at me.

Leaving my jeans undone, I crawled onto the bed before I could stop myself.

Aiden's head snapped up, his beautiful blue eyes widening a touch.

Ripping his phone from his hand, I tossed it onto the nightstand and shoved him back. "I just…I need…" I swallowed a curse. I had never been one to not have something to say. I got that trait from my father. But Aiden had me unraveled. With his nervous energy and his broad chest rising and falling with ragged breaths, I couldn't help but soak it up.

As if he got the hint, Aiden cupped the back of my neck and pulled me down to meet the rough impact of his mouth.

I didn't have time to dwell on it as his tongue slipped between my lips and his hands began roaming over my torso. He pushed me onto my back, broke the kiss, and ripped open my jeans.

As much as I needed to be in control, I needed this more. Not sex. That would happen when he was truly ready but a release of some kind would help. My skin vibrated, the rage rushing through me like a damn drug.

Aiden bent over my waist, placing a soft peck on my hip bone before he sunk his teeth into the flesh there.

The sweet pain forced a yelp from my lips.

He only grinned, licking along the spot he bit to soothe the sting.

My hands clutched the blankets beneath me, my hips bucking up.

Thankfully, I didn't have to wait long for more as he reached into my jeans and pulled out my cock.

Wrapping a hand around the thick length, he lowered his mouth and sucked me to the back of his throat.

I groaned, my eyes rolling into the back of my head.

Aiden gagged around me but he didn't stop. He worked up a rhythm, stroking and licking, slurping and damn near sucking my soul right out of me. He had mentioned that he had never messed around with a guy before me so for someone who was new to giving head, he sucked cock like a damn pro.

Sliding my fingers into his hair, our eyes locked.

His lips were pulled tight while his mouth was stuffed with my dick.

"Brace yourself," I told him, planting my feet on the bed.

He took a deep breath, his nostrils flaring at my demand.

Tightening my hold on his hair, I began lifting my hips up and down.

The sounds of him gagging only made me fuck his throat harder and faster. Spittle leaked out of the corners his mouth; tears dripping down his cheeks. That was the only thing I needed to set me off. Holding his head, I pulled him down the length of my cock, his mouth reaching the base of me as my release poured down his throat.

"Fuck," I shouted out, trying everything I could to bring him closer.

Aiden moaned, the vibration sending a jolt of pleasure shooting down my spine.

When I calmed down, I released him.

He wiped his face and gave me a crooked grin.

I chuckled, breathing through the erratic beating of my heart.

"Better?" he asked, licking his lips.

"I know I'm your first but, Aiden, you suck cock like it's your damn job." I sat up and placed a soft peck on his mouth. "I feel like I should pay you."

A laugh boomed through him. "Well…thank you." He paused. "I've never actually done that before. I haven't done any of the stuff we've done." His cheeks turned pink and I wasn't ashamed to say, it turned me on.

"I'm honored that I'm your first," I murmured, running my thumb along his bottom lip.

His breath caught, his deep blue eyes darkening the longer time went on where we didn't speak.

"You seemed stressed," he told me. "So, I was trying to make you feel better."

My heart stuttered at his confession.

"Did it help?" he asked gently.

My dick twitched at the innocence seeping from him. He had said that he wasn't a virgin by any means, but it made me wonder just how much experience he actually had. Or if he was just that submissive when it came to me. One could only hope.

I moved to the head of the bed and leaned back against the headboard. "It helped." Patting the spot beside me, I waited. I had work to do and I really needed to head to my store, but at the moment this was more important.

Aiden did as instructed and slipped beneath the covers, moving to the empty space beside me.

"I want you to know something." I turned to him, giving him my full attention and needing his just the same. "I like you. A lot. I feel comfortable with you. Sure, I have more experience when it comes to sex but none of that matters. I want to learn what you like. What you don't like. And I'll make it my mission to help you feel safe and secure with me."

"You mean that?" he asked, searching my face. For a sign. For something. For a lie that he would never see because I only spoke the truth. My father had taught me to communicate with my partners. Sometimes I said too much and my mouth got away from me quite often, but at least the people I messed around with knew exactly where they stood with me.

"I do mean that, Aiden. I mean it more than I could ever tell you."

He looked down at his hands resting in his lap. "I'm hungry."

I frowned, tilting my head. "My cock didn't satisfy that hunger?"

When his eyes connected with mine, a slow grin spread on his face. "Oh, it did but I'm hungry for actual food. So…" He cleared his throat. "Would you want to go on a date? With me?"

Ripping the covers off of us, I moved to the spot between his legs. "Yes, absolutely I want to go on a date with you. But first." I looked down at his thick cock. "I need something to hold me over."

TWELVE

AIDEN

ROWAN DROVE US TO a small deli that was open twenty-four seven. While we sat in a booth across from each other, I couldn't help but think about his mouth that had been wrapped around my cock only a half hour before.

Pretending to scan the menu, my thoughts were only about him. His lips. His tongue. His hand gripping the shaft of my length while he had sucked me deep into his mouth.

A shiver raced down my spine.

Rowan coughed.

I glanced up, meeting his gaze across the table.

"Something wrong?" he asked, his eyes dropping to my mouth.

"Nope," I croaked.

He chuckled, sitting back in the booth and running his fingers along his lips. "What are you thinking about?"

"Nothing." I drew in a deep breath. "Nothing at all."

His laugh deepened, forcing a smile on my face.

Scanning the menu once again, I flipped through the pages and noticed how there were no drinks besides milkshakes, water, and your standard juices and sodas. "There's no alcohol."

"Nope, there isn't."

"Did you specifically choose this place for that reason?" I asked him, placing the menu back on the table.

"I did." He gave me a small smile.

My heart jumped, my palms suddenly became sweaty. I appreciated the gesture, but I suddenly felt backed into a corner as a result of it and I wasn't sure why. You would think that I would be happy that there was no alcohol. That there was no temptation. But maybe that was the problem. Maybe I needed the temptation so I could choose if I would fight it or not.

"Aiden?"

Squeezing my eyes shut, I shook my head and took a deep breath.

The spot beside me suddenly dipped. When a warm hand covered mine that was resting in my lap, I slowly blinked my eyes open.

"I'm sorry," Rowan whispered, his mouth pressed gently against my ear. "I didn't think."

"It's okay." I linked my fingers in his, holding his hand tight in mine. "Thank you. For this. It's still weird though. I'm not used to people being considerate of my…" I swallowed hard. "Addiction." People around me tried to understand and acted like they did but they never truly got it. They didn't get the constant struggle. They didn't get how I couldn't have just one drink and that be it. They didn't get how I actually psychically *needed* to drown myself in a bottle.

"Maybe it's because they're not used to being around it," Rowan offered. "My mom is an alcoholic and my dad is a drug addict. He doesn't drink either. He says it's safer that way."

I looked up at him then when his words stopped.

"I just want you to know that while I may not understand exactly what you're going through, I've been around it my whole entire life." His hand squeezed mine. "You're not alone, Aiden. At all."

"I know." I pulled my hand out from under his and linked our fingers. Grazing my thumb over the back of his hand, I found myself wondering what it would be like to be with him. To truly be with him. To feel his rough calloused hands running all over my body. To feel him deep inside me as he claimed what I had never given to someone before. Would it be rough? Fast or slow? Gentle? Just from the foreplay we shared between us, I was betting that sex with Rowan would be something I could never prepare myself for. No matter how much I tried.

I was vaguely aware of Rowan ordering some food for us, along with a milkshake each. When the food arrived, my mouth watered at the large plate of french fries.

Placing his hand on my inner thigh, Rowan gripped me tight. Almost like he was silently telling me that he wasn't going anywhere. No matter how closed up I was, he would always be there.

"You can never go wrong with french fries," he said, breaking the comfortable silence.

"You really can't. It's perfect hangover food too." Not that I had been hungover a lot. I usually just kept on drinking in that case, which was dangerous all on its own.

"I'm not a drinker, so I wouldn't know, but with the grease and salt, it makes sense."

I shifted in my seat, my muscles jumping beneath my skin. I tried eating but I couldn't taste anything. I even took a sip of the milkshake but it had no flavor. What the hell was wrong with me?

"Aiden." Rowan turned his big body toward me, shielding me from any onlookers.

"Can I get you anything else?" I heard the waitress ask.

"Not right now," Rowan replied, his voice curt. "Take a deep breath, baby," he murmured.

"I can't do this," I said instead, not listening to him.

"Deep breath," he repeated. "*Now.*"

A hot shiver raced down my spine at his rough demand.

"Why are you here?" I asked him, knowing full well he would be pissed that I didn't listen to him when he told me to stop saying that this was too fast. "Why do you want to do…" I waved out a hand in front of me. "…this?"

"Because if you haven't noticed, I like you. I invited you into my bed the first night you moved in." Rowan cupped my cheek, turning my head around to face him. "Whether you believe in it or not, something brought us together."

"You invited me into your bed that first night because you felt sorry for me." As soon as I said the words, I regretted them.

Rowan pulled away, signalling for the waitress. "Can we get the bill and a container to put these fries in please?"

"Of course." She placed the bill on the table and rushed off to grab a container for the leftover food like Rowan requested.

"We can eat these here," I told him. "We don't have to leave."

He shot me a look that made my heart jump in my chest. It was a look that told me to shut the hell up, but I found that I didn't want to. I wanted him unhinged, pissed off, and ready to tear me apart. I wanted to experience that anger and let it slide over my skin like I wanted his hands to do the same.

"We're leaving," was all he said as he threw some cash on the table and left the booth.

When the waitress came back, I quickly packed up the fries and rushed out of the deli to find Rowan.

"Rowan?" I stopped, looked around me, but wasn't able to see him anywhere. Did he leave? My heart sunk. Rubbing the back of my neck, I let out a harsh sigh. I clearly fucked up.

It was a mild evening, so I decided to walk the few blocks it took to get home. Maybe it would give us both time to calm down and let me think about what the hell I had said that could piss him off. I didn't have a lot of experience when it came to relationships, but I had seen the possessiveness come out in my brother and the people we had grown up with. Being on the receiving end of it was something I wasn't used to. Not that I was ever overly the dominant type anyway.

I sent Rowan a quick text, telling him I was sorry and that I was walking home. I also suggested that if he needed space, I could find somewhere else to spend the night. About a minute after I sent that text, the hairs on the back of my neck tingled.

A firm hand suddenly wrapped around my arm, pulling me into a nearby alleyway. Before I knew what was happening, I was shoved up against a wall.

"You are not spending the night anywhere else but in my bed," a deep voice growled in my ear.

My body came alive at Rowan being so close. "It was just a suggestion."

"Shut the fuck up." When he pressed his waist into the seat of my ass, all breath left me. "You keep questioning why I want to be with you, why I like you, why I want to fucking date you, and it's pissing me off." He spun me around, grabbed my hands, and pulled my arms above my head in a rough move. "I'm going to tell you this again. I've been around and I may be more experienced than you but that means shit when this is new. It's new for me and it's new for you. I'm patient. Maybe too patient. But I like you and I'll keep telling you that I like you until it sinks in. I like going to bed with you and I like knowing that you'll be there in the morning. The next time you tell me that you're going to spend the night somewhere else, I won't stop you, but I promise that I *will* find you."

My dick twitched at the threat hidden beneath his words.

Rowan tilted his head, his dark eyes searing into me. "Tell me what you want. One thing. Anything at all. Something that you've never had before. And I'll do everything in my fucking power to give it to you."

I swallowed hard, licking my parched lips. "You."

THIRTEEN

ROWAN

I PRACTICALLY DRAGGED AIDEN out of that alley and to my car. He didn't object and only followed me like the good little submissive he was. His willingness to comply set my body on edge. He needed something and I was damn willing to give it to him.

It had been a long time for me and I knew right away that I wouldn't be gentle. Not as much as I should. Especially when he had never been with a man before. He sure as hell was going to remember this night, since it would be his first time being fucked in the ass. A shiver slid over my skin, the tiny hairs on my body tingling with anticipation over what was to come.

Once we reached my vehicle, I spun on him. "I will do anything you want. I will fulfill any desires you have. Any fantasies. Anything at all, Aiden." I was losing my ever-loving mind over this man. This beautiful, broken man. He stood only a foot away, but it felt like a universe sat between us.

"I just want you," he murmured, his voice soft.

"No." I closed the distance between us and gripped the back of his neck. "Louder. Say what you want."

"I want you," his voice came out louder that time, but it wasn't enough. I needed to know that he was serious because once I had him, I knew I would never be able to let him go. No matter how much he pushed me away and needed that damn space, he would be it for me.

"Again." I spun us around, slamming him up against the side of my car. "Louder."

Aiden's pupils dilated. Even in the dim lighting of the parking lot, I could see it. He liked when I was unraveled.

"I want you, Rowan. I want whatever you're willing to offer me."

"Everything, Aiden." I inhaled a deep breath, trying to get control of these feelings rushing through me. "I will offer you everything."

Before any more words slid between us, he cupped my head and pulled my mouth down to his. The rough impact forced a growl from the back of my throat.

Aiden ran his hands beneath my shirt, around to my back, and pulled me closer. When our waists touched, I pushed into him even more.

He broke the kiss, trailing his mouth down the length of my jaw. "I want you to fuck me," he whispered against my ear. "I want you to be my first."

"Aiden." I captured his head in my hands, forcing him to look me square in the eye. "I'll be your fucking everything."

Sure, it was too soon to go down *that* road, but I meant what I said. The universe had us meet for a reason. Whether he wanted to believe it or not, this was meant to be.

Before he could question me again, I pulled away from him and stomped around to the driver's side. "Get in." I was damn near vibrating out of my skin with need for this man.

As soon as Aiden was seated beside me and had the door closed, I peeled out of the driveway. The tires squealed, knocking us around harder than I expected, but I needed him. I needed to know him. Every inch of him.

I reached out my hand, also needing his touch.

When his fingers slid between mine, I placed his hand on my crotch. "This is yours, Aiden. Anytime you want it, you take it."

His breath catching made me continue.

"All of this is also going to be inside of you very soon because fuck, baby, I can't wait anymore."

"I need to know what you feel like." He cupped my dick over my pants, massaging his palm against me. "I need to know how rough you are. What you like. What you don't like. I need it all, Rowan."

A shiver raced down my spine at the pleasure shooting through every inch of me.

Pressing my foot on the gas, I sped up, forcing a deep chuckle from Aiden. The sound tingled through my balls.

"It's going to hurt," I told him.

"Fuck, that's what I'm hoping for."

His words had been so soft, I wasn't sure I heard him correctly.

When we were finally at our apartment, I quickly left the vehicle.

Aiden did the same but only stood there as I went up to him. His deep blue eyes connected with mine, a light shade of pink sat in his cheeks. He was damn near breathtaking and I couldn't wait to make him yell out my name.

Locking the car, I grabbed his hand and rushed us to the old building. When we were in the elevator, I had him against the wall and my mouth on his before he could take his next breath.

"Rowan," he whispered, his body arching as I roamed my hands up his torso.

When the elevator doors dinged open, I pulled away from Aiden, checking out my handiwork. His hair was a mess, his clothes wrinkled, and his cheeks were even redder, but he was hot as *fuck*.

"Apartment. *Now.*" I wanted to go slow for him, but I couldn't. I knew in advance that I couldn't. Thankfully I had a lot of lube in stock because I didn't want to hurt him even though he said he wanted me to.

Aiden stepped out in the hall, making his way to our apartment.

I followed him.

Once we stopped outside our door, I already had my shirt off and my jeans undone. When he noticed that I was half naked, his nostrils flared.

"Get the fuck in the apartment, Aiden."

He unlocked the door and did as he was told, I stayed back for a few. I needed to catch my breath. But I knew, Lord did I ever know, this was going to change us. And I couldn't wait to see just how much he could take.

(Aiden)

As soon as I stepped over that threshold, I was shoved from behind. A heavy hand grabbed what little hair I had, pulling my head back.

"Keep walking," Rowan practically growled.

While he wasn't that much taller than me, whenever he got like this, it made him appear ten times bigger than he actually was. Maybe that was the point. I wasn't sure, as it was new for me, but I liked it just the same.

"Undo your jeans and take out your cock. I want to see how hard you are for me."

I did as I was told, a low hiss leaving me as my fingers wrapped around my thick shaft.

"Hmm…" Rowan slapped my hand away, replacing my fingers with his own. He tugged and pulled, forcing sounds from my mouth I had never heard leave me before.

When we finally reached the bedroom, he released me completely and pushed me inside.

"Strip."

That single word made my knees shake. Looked like I was more submissive than I thought I would be.

As soon as I had my shirt off, I was once again shoved from behind.

Rowan bent me over the edge of the bed, helping me rip my jeans and boxers over my ass and down my thighs. A hard swat landed on my ass cheek, pulling a moan from the back of my throat. He repeated the movement, my skin stinging at the impact.

When he pulled away from me, I turned my head and watched him go to the nightstand. He went through the items the top drawer, pulling out a bottle of lube and a box of condoms. The items he was holding sent a shiver down my spine, knowing that this was it. There was no going back now.

"Tell me you're sure," he said, his voice rough.

"I'm sure." I breathed.

"Tell me you want me to fuck you." He gazed my way, his eyes connecting with mine. "Say it."

"I want you to fuck me."

Rowan came up behind me, placing the items on the bed and pulling my jeans and boxers off the rest of the way. When he closed the distance between us, he pushed his cock between the cheeks of my ass.

My breath hitched, my fingers tightening around the blankets beneath me.

"You feel that, baby boy? That's going to be in your ass. I can't wait either. I bet you're tight as fuck." Rowan gripped my hips, undulating against me.

My breathing picked up, my body shaking.

"Rowan." I moaned, pushing my ass back into his touch.

"It's been so fucking long." He landed another swat on my ass, the impact making me stop moving. "Fucking hell, I love how responsive you are. You listen so well, Aiden. You're such a good boy."

The praise coming from him, made my dick lengthen even more.

"Keep your face pressed against the bed and don't move." Rowan ran a finger down the length of my spine, the sound of a bottle opening a moment later.

I did as I was told, waiting with bated breath for the next step. The next moment in our relationship, if you could even call it that.

Something cold suddenly dripped between the cheeks of my ass. My heart jumped, my hands tightening around the blankets beneath me.

"Shhh…" Rowan leaned over me, placing a soft peck on my shoulder. "I got you, Aiden. Anything I do that you don't like, just tell me." A tinfoil package sounded a moment later, followed by the head of his cock, brushing against my opening. It sparked a need for more. "I know I should prep you but fuck, Aiden, I want my cock to be the first thing you feel."

"Do it. Please."

He repeated the movements, running the lube over the tight rim. He pushed against me every so often, the movement forcing him to enter me a little more each time.

"Rowan." I arched beneath him, needing him to hurry up. "Please. I need *you*."

He grunted, gently nipping my neck at the same time as he shoved himself inside of me in a quick thrust.

I shouted out.

He groaned.

I was damn thankful for that lube because I was sure if we didn't have it, it would burn even more. But he never did let me get used to the size of him.

Rowan grabbed my hips, leaned back, and started fucking me.

"Oh, fuck," I practically sobbed. It felt like he was trying to split me in half. I was sure that most would just start with a finger or two, or even a butt plug but he was right, I needed his cock to be the first thing I felt too.

The harder he fucked me, the higher the pleasure rose. Even with all of the women I had been with, none of those moments felt like this.

"Yes, that's it. Take my dick, Aiden. It's filling you up so good." He pounded into me, the burn from before soon replaced with a pleasure so great, spots danced in my vision. I felt full and it still burned, but at the same time it was exactly what I had needed.

"Take it," he yelled, digging his fingers into my hips.

I slammed back into him, taking his cock even deeper.

"Yes, just like that. You like that ass filled with cock, don't you, baby boy?"

I whimpered, kept the side of my face pressed against the bed, and gave into his savagery.

Rowan towered over me, pushing his dick into me as deep as my body would allow. "Does knowing my cock fills your tight little ass, make you feel better, Aiden?"

"Yes," I whispered.

He covered my hand, linking his fingers between mine. "I'm your first, Aiden."

While I had lost my virginity to a woman years ago, this was different. They say you never forget your first and I knew that no matter what happened between Rowan and me, I would never forget this. No matter how much I tried.

FOURTEEN

ROWAN

JUST OVER AN HOUR later and I was still inside of Aiden. We were now lying on our sides and I was fucking him from behind. With my hand wrapped around his throat and my cock deep in his ass, it forced these sexy as fuck sounds to leave his mouth.

I could have gone longer. I could have spent hours inside of him. He was safe in my arms and I needed him to know that. If I was a gentleman, I would have given him some sort of reprieve but when he begged me not to stop, I listened.

Sliding my hand down the length of his body, I circled my fingers around his swollen dick. He had already come twice, but I still never stopped. He would learn rather quickly that I could go for hours without having an orgasm.

"Please come," he moaned. "Please, Rowan. I can't take any more."

"Not until you do." I tugged at his cock, forcing loud whimpers to leave him. When warm spurts of liquid coated my hand, I finally gave in to the pleasure. After a few more thrusts, my dick swelled, my release pouring into the condom. *"Fuuuuuck."*

When we both calmed down, I gently pulled from his body, ripped off the condom, and tied it off before placing it in the trash.

Lying back down beside Aiden, I pulled him into my arms. "You good?"

"Oh yeah." He yawned, shivering against me.

Running my hand up and down the length of his arm, I placed a soft peck on his shoulder. "Are you sure? Did I hurt you at all?"

Aiden sat up and turned on the lamp. "You have no idea what you've just done for me."

I moved to the spot beside him, curling the blankets up and around our laps. We should probably change the sheets, but I didn't really care about that. My bed now smelled like him, and it was a scent I wanted to stay there forever. "What do you mean?"

When he looked away, his jaw clenched. "I think I've always felt like I had to be with women because my brother was. He would bring them home and I joined in because I thought it was normal. But after, it never felt normal to me. This…what we just shared…" Aiden still wouldn't meet my gaze, but he grabbed my hand and placed it in his lap. "It's the most normal I've ever felt. It was right. It was everything I wanted and needed."

"You've mentioned several times how this is fast," I said gently, keeping my voice low so as not to spook him from speaking any more of his thoughts. "But I'm not expecting marriage here, Aiden. I just want you. I want every second with you. Every hour. Day. Month. And we can go from there."

"One day at a time," he whispered.

"No." I cupped his cheek, turning his head to face me. "One moment at a time. Okay?"

He nodded. "Okay."

"Good." I pulled away from him and left the bed. "Let's take a shower." When I turned around, Aiden muttered a curse. "Like what you see?" I chuckled.

"Oh yeah." Aiden left the bed and came up to me, his flaccid cock bouncing between his powerful thighs.

"I like what I see too." And fuck me did I ever. He was hard in all the right places. Working in construction did wonders for his form.

"I know." He closed the distance between us, wrapping his arms around my middle and placing a soft peck on my cheek. "You couldn't get enough of my ass."

"Why, Aiden. Are you flirting with me?"

He winked and kissed my cheek one more time before he pulled away and left the bedroom.

Once I was alone, I ran a hand through my hair and blew out a slow breath. I had no idea what I was doing but there was one person who could help.

I needed to talk to my sister.

The following afternoon, I was on my way to my sister's place, but I couldn't help but think back to the night before. After Aiden and I took a shower, we made something to eat and ended up watching a few movies. It was comfortable being around him. I didn't have to be on all of the time like a lot of people expected. I said what was on my mind, usually had no filter, and sometimes had a sick sense of humor. I got that from my father. When I said something that shouldn't even be considered remotely funny, Aiden would laugh and shake his head.

I realized then that it was a sound I wanted to hear and often.

As I pulled up in front of my sister and brother-in-law's place, I texted Aiden and let him know where I was. I had dropped him off at a friend's place, our conversation before he left my car, not sitting well with me.

"I won't drink," Aiden told me, opening the passenger side door.

"Why do you feel the need to tell me that?"

"Don't I have to?"

"*Aiden, alcoholism is a disease. It's one that will never go away, and you'll struggle with it for the rest of your life. But if you relapse, I'll be there. Every step of the way with you.*"

"*Why?*" He frowned. "*The people who are supposed to love me, wouldn't even be there every step of the way with me.*"

I was sure they had their own reasons, so it wasn't overly fair for Aiden to make that assumption. But I didn't know his parents or brother or his friends. It made me wonder why he insisted on going to this little get-together in the first place when he was adamant all along that it made him uncomfortable.

"*I don't know what to say to that,*" I confessed.

"*It's fine.*" Aiden leaned over and placed a soft peck on my mouth. "*I'll see you later.*"

Scrubbing a hand down my face, I let out a harsh sigh and gave myself a shake. Aiden would learn to understand that I was patient. Especially when it came to him.

Leaving the car, I walked up the driveway. Once I reached the front door, it opened before I could knock.

"It's about time you show up," Pearson, my brother-in-law muttered.

"Yeah, yeah." I closed the distance between us and gave him a hug.

He chuckled, returning the embrace. "How are you doing?"

"Oh, not too bad." I shrugged. "Just stopped by to see my sister. The boys here?"

"They're actually at your parents' place." Pearson stepped to the side, letting me enter his house.

"Am I interrupting a date night?" Having two boys under six, they didn't get a lot of time alone. So, I didn't want to take that away from them if I could help it.

"We have dinner reservations in an hour, so you have time if you need to talk to Ettie." Pearson ran a hand through his auburn shaggy hair. I had never been into redheads but even I had to admit that my brother-in-law was hot as hell. Especially with the tattoos that covered most of his exposed skin. They made him appear mean and look like a biker, when really, he was a big teddy bear. At least for his wife and kids he was.

"I thought I heard voices." Ettie came down the hall and into the living room.

"I won't stay long," I told her, holding out my arms. "Just needed to talk to you."

"Oh?" She raised an eyebrow. "Everything okay?" she asked, coming into my arms.

I hugged her, maybe a little longer than normal but I needed my older sister at the moment.

"Rowan?" She leaned back, looking up at me but keeping her arms around my waist.

"I'll give you two some privacy." Pearson kissed his wife on top of the head before disappearing down the hall.

"Talk to me." Ettie lightly patted my chest. "You can tell me anything."

"I know." I stepped out of her embrace and walked across the living room to the patio doors that led out into the backyard. "I don't know how to start I guess."

"Start from the middle."

I looked at her then.

Ettie only shrugged, the movement making her chestnut brown curls brush her shoulders. "Everyone says to start from the beginning, I was trying to be different."

She *was* different. That was what I loved about her and obviously what Pearson loved about her as well.

"I slept with my roommate and he's an alcoholic and I'm also the first guy he's ever been with, but I want to have a relationship with him and could see myself also falling in love with him," I blurted all in one breath.

A mixture of emotions passed over my sister's face. Shock, bewilderment, pity. I wasn't sure which one of them was directed at me. Probably shock. Maybe not.

"I know." I shoved my hands in my pockets. "It's fucked up."

"Let's go out back." Ettie opened the patio door and led the way outside. I followed her because I needed the big sisterly advice that she was so good at giving me.

"Do *you* think I fucked up?" I slumped onto a patio chair and ran a hand through my hair. "I like him," I confessed before she could answer. "I like him a lot. He's quiet but he's comfortable to be around."

My sister sat on the couch beside me. "You're happy?"

"I am. The happiest I've ever been but he has severe PTSD. I don't know what happened, but I do know that it caused him to fall into the bottle." I wished Aiden would talk to me, but I would have to be patient.

"Then the only thing I can suggest is to be patient with him like Mom was patient with Dad. And she's still patient with him to this day." Ettie shook her head. "It amazes me. Their love."

"You have the same with Pearson," I pointed out.

"I do." She smiled. "But I wish the same for you too."

"Maybe I don't deserve it." Lord knew I didn't always have a legal job. Case in point, Miguel Sincero.

"How has this guy been with you?"

"Aiden's been everything that I need." I sat forward, scrubbing my hand down my face. "I don't know. He hasn't let me in. His walls are fucking high. But I want him to let me in. Even if it's slowly and only a bit at a time."

"Wow." She laughed lightly. "I've never seen you like this. With anyone at all."

I went to argue and tell her that there had been someone else who affected me like this but when I thought about it, really thought about it, I realized that my sister was right. I had liked Miguel at a time when I needed him. I was still ashamed of the fact that I had used him. I should have read the signs and paid attention to how unstable he was. Maybe then he wouldn't currently be stalking me.

"I don't know what to do," I muttered.

"Be patient," Ettie said gently. "If you like him as much as you say you do, then you need to give him time. Especially when he's been through a lot."

"I just want him to talk to me." While I wanted to know every single thing about him, I was nervous at the same time to find out all of his dark and dirty secrets. Could I handle his truths?

"I think you can."

My head whipped around, finding my sister smiling at me. I didn't realize I had spoken out loud.

"Does he know your truths?"

I nodded.

"Then I think you can handle his." She gently nudged me in the shoulder. "Does he know about Miguel?"

I nodded again.

"And he took it well?"

"He did. Better than I thought he would." My sister had been the only one I'd ever told about Miguel and how he had paid me for sex in the beginning. He didn't always pay me but that was how it started out. She never judged me and she said that as long we both consented to it, who cared? But I did. Not because I was being paid for sexual favors but because I should have put an end to it when the alarm bells started going off before we even had sex. Miguel had been borderline stalkerish from the very beginning but I had been lonely, so I never turned him down. I also needed the money which didn't help make matters any easier at the time.

"I think I need to just reassure him that I'm not going anywhere."

Ettie nodded. "That's a good idea."

"Thank you." I stood, holding out my arms.

"I didn't really do anything." She laughed, walking into my outstretched arms. "But you're welcome."

"You did more than you know." And that was the truth.

We left the backyard arm in arm and headed back into the house.

"I'll let you finish getting ready for your date." I gave my sister another hug. We said our goodbyes and I left the house.

Checking my phone, I saw that I had no new texts or voicemails from Aiden. Not that I expected it. He wasn't a man of many words. But I did notice a voicemail from an unknown number. Sending a brief text, I quickly made my way back to my car. Just as I sat in the driver's seat, a text came in.

My stomach twisted.

Instead of responding, I dialed up the number.

"I was wondering when you would call me," came a deep reply.

"What the hell do you want, Miguel?" I wished there had been a way that I could make this man see that I wasn't good for him. He needed to move on. I never made him believe that we could have more. He was living in a fantasy world and I wasn't sure how to convince him otherwise.

"You know what I want, Rowan."

There had been a time where the silky voice would have set my blood on fire but not so much anymore. He was too damn clingy. I didn't go for that shit.

"You paid me for a service. I gave it to you. End of."

"We're good together, Rowan. Even after I stopped paying you. We were perfect for each other."

"We really weren't. You deserve so much better, Miguel."

"I…Baby, I just…"

My chest tightened over the hurt in his deep voice. I didn't want this. I never meant to break his heart. "Please forget me."

"I can't," he whispered.

My back stiffened. "What do you want?"

"You, Rowan. I just want you."

FIFTEEN

ROWAN

THIS WAS NOT HAPPENING.

I had been known to be a lot of things, but I would not fall victim to this shit.

"You can't have me, Miguel." My fingers tightened around my phone. "That was never the deal. You knew that from the very beginning."

"Yeah, you see, I've actually changed my mind. You know how that is, don't you, Rowan? One moment you want something and then you change your mind, and you end up wanting something else? I know you know how that is."

"If you're referring to my sexual preferences, which in fact is none of your business, you can fuck right off." Once I was seated in the driver's side of my car, I pulled the phone away from my ear. I thought maybe Miguel had hung up with the seconds that ticked on where he didn't say anything.

"Does he know? Does he know that I paid you for cyber sex? Does he know that once we actually met, I still paid you to fuck me?"

My jaw clenched. It had been a kink of his and one, to this day, I regretted falling for. "Actually, Miguel. I did tell him, and he didn't judge me. Not one bit."

"You're lying," he whispered.

"Listen, as much as I'm really enjoying this conversation, I have shit to do. So, if you're not going to tell me exactly what you want, I'm going to hang up."

"I'll be in touch, Rowan." Miguel hung up before I could, leaving me to stew in my own thoughts.

Slamming a palm against the steering wheel, I let out a string of curse words that would make my father blush. I didn't like being backed into a corner and I definitely sure as hell didn't like not being in control.

Just when I was about to fire up the car and head to my store before I had to pick Aiden up, my phone rang again.

"Listen, fucker," I answered without checking the call display.

"Um…I'm sorry. Is this Rowan?" came a female voice.

"Who the fuck is this and how did you get this number?" I was sick of this shit. I hadn't slept with a lot of women but if there was someone else coming to demand something from me, I was going to burn the fucking world down.

"Wow, do you kiss your mama with that mouth?" The woman laughed.

"Who is this?" I bit out, not having patience for this.

"This is Meadow. I'm looking for Aiden. His brother said that he could be with you because you're roommates now or something, so he gave me your number to call."

"Looking for Aiden," I repeated. "Why are you looking for Aiden?" Warning bells went off in my head. Something was wrong.

"He was supposed to come over for a little get-together I'm throwing. I asked Ashton if he heard from him, and he hasn't. He told me to call you."

Aiden had given his brother and his parents my number in case of emergencies. Normally I would have said no but when Aiden didn't drive and with there being this connection between us, I didn't mind. Not like they knew the people I was trying to ignore anyway.

"I dropped Aiden off at a house. I'm assuming it was yours then if you're hosting this little get-together."

"Well…he's not here."

My chest tightened, my stomach twisting.

"And he's not answering his phone or replying to my text messages," she added.

"I dropped him off," I repeated.

"Where did you drop him off?"

I gave Meadow the address Aiden had given me.

"Rowan…" She paused. "That's not my address."

What the hell was going on?

"I'll call you back." I disconnected the call and dialed up Aiden. I expected to get his voicemail, so when he answered, it threw me off. But he didn't say anything. I could hear him breathing and that was it.

"Aiden? What's going on?" I asked him gently, not needing him to hang up only to disappear for good.

"I wanted to be alone," he murmured, his voice thick with emotion that I could feel down to the pit of my soul. "I…I just…"

"What? Talk to me." Did something happen between the time I dropped him off and now? Was he that damn good of an actor, that he had been on the verge of losing it all day and I just didn't notice?

"I don't want to be alone anymore."

"Tell me where you are." I fired up the car and sped down the street, needing to get to the man who was currently losing himself.

"I'm lost. I'm so fucking lost."

"I got you, baby. Tell me where you are, and I'll help you find whatever it is that you need." I wasn't sure if that would help but it was the truth. Maybe I was taking on more baggage than necessary. But I realized something, especially when Aiden answered my call and not Meadow's. I could only assume that Ashton had tried contacting him as well, so when Aiden picked up for me, it set everything in stone. I was falling for him.

"I'm on a cliff," Aiden said, letting out a harsh sigh.

The hackles on the back of my neck rose. "Please stay there. Tell me where you are, and I'll come to you. If you need to stay there all night, we will. But please don't do anything. I just need to know where you are."

When Aiden finally gave me his location, I breathed out a sigh of relief and made my way to him. I wasn't sure how he got to where he currently was in such a short time. Maybe he hitchhiked or took a cab. Either way, I was on my way to him and I would help him through whatever it was that was bothering him. No matter what and no matter the cost. Miguel could go fuck himself. Aiden was who I wanted. No. He was who I *needed*.

"Stay on the phone with me, Aiden," I instructed, listening to the sound of his breathing.

"I'm sorry."

"Don't be sorry." I didn't like this side of him. "I'm heading your way, Aiden. Whatever you need, I'll give it to you and if I can't give it to you, I'll do everything in my fucking power to make sure you have it. I promise."

He didn't respond but he didn't hang up either. I was fine with that. I made sure to listen to his breathing as I neared where he was. A little while later and I was out of town and driving down a gravel road with rows of trees on either side of it.

Once I reached a clearing, I saw him. He was standing at the edge of a cliff, not moving but still making me nervous with how close he was to falling. One step in the wrong direction and everything could end.

Disconnecting the call, I crept the car slowly toward him and came to a stop a few feet back. Killing the engine, I tried my best to quietly get out of the car. Careful not to spook him, I closed the door just enough that it would latch.

Taking a deep breath, I walked toward him. Once I was standing beside him, I followed his line of sight. The cliff overlooked the town. A town I had spent the last few years in just to get out of the city. Although I was still close enough that it didn't take overly long to visit my family, it was far enough that it didn't feel like I was living in a big city. It had been what I needed for a long time even though some people were trying their hardest to take that away from me.

"I led my squad into an ambush."

My head whipped around, not expecting Aiden to say anything. When he didn't meet my gaze and only looked straight ahead, I turned back around and listened.

SIXTEEN

AIDEN

"WE WERE IN A Humvee. A group of us were followed by several others. We were heading into friendly territory or that was what we were told anyway. I saw a kid coming out into the street. He was only in a diaper and much too old to be wearing one, but I don't judge. They have it hard over there." I sucked in a sharp breath, baring all of my truths. Truths I had never told anyone. I told my brother a bit of what had happened but not everything. I wasn't sure why. Maybe I thought he would judge me or blame me for what had happened. Even though it wasn't my fault and I didn't have any control over the situation, it didn't lessen this guilt at all. It had weighed heavily on my shoulders for months now and the only way to lift it even just a little, was by submitting to the one vice that would eventually kill me.

"I shouldn't have gone up to him, but I did," I continued. "I found out later on that he was a decoy. Next thing I knew, explosions started, shots were fired, and then everything went black. I woke up to the sounds of screaming and other noises I don't want to think about or know where they were coming from. The girls, my Navy sisters, were raped and tortured. I don't know why they chose me to survive. But…I did, and I regret it. Every damn day I regret it."

Calloused fingers slipped between mine. It was a gentle touch, but it forced some strength into me. Strength I felt I didn't deserve.

"I could have stayed in the Navy if I would have talked to someone. It was a stipulation, but I couldn't. I didn't want to talk about it." I drew in a sharp breath. "I still don't. Not with anyone else but you." I looked up at Rowan then. The sun was setting, and it cast a shadow over him. It was eerie in a way how close we had become in such a short time. No matter what happened between us though, I would forever be grateful to him for everything he had done for me. He taught me that it was okay to be myself. That it was okay to not know exactly what I wanted and to experiment. He taught me that it was okay to not want sex. A shaky sigh left me, suddenly wishing I could take back all of my words.

"I'm sorry," he finally said. "I'm sorry for what you went through. For surviving when others didn't. I'm sorry for your Navy family. For their families. But I'm not sorry that you're here. Maybe it's selfish of me. But I'm glad you're here." He slipped an arm around my back, pulling me closer. "Really glad and I know your parents, brother, and friends are glad as well."

"I'm…" Was I thankful that I was still around when others from my team weren't? "I've tried committing suicide," I blurted, my eyes widening at my confession. "I've never said that out loud before." It had been a truth, a dark truth, I had kept to myself. Ashton had asked me after my accident if I had tried killing myself and if that was the reason I had driven drunk. I told him I wasn't sure when in all reality, it had definitely been the case. I just never cared to admit it.

"You've been through a lot, Aiden," Rowan said gently. "Were there any other survivors?"

"Not from my team, no."

"Have you tried reaching out to the families?"

"I…" A memory suddenly hit me.

"How could you? How could you lead my baby into that hell?" the woman screamed, spittle flying from her mouth. "What makes you so damn special that they saved you?"

"I haven't reached out to them since but it's…I blame myself. They had a big funeral for everyone we lost. I stayed back. I couldn't deal with anyone else blaming me. I did that enough on my own." Lord knew I needed counseling or something but talking to Rowan, surprisingly, eased some of the heavy weight off of my shoulders.

"It's not your fault, Aiden, but I understand why you would feel like it is. It doesn't matter what I say though. *You* have to believe it."

I looked up at him, expecting to find judgement written in the lines on his handsome face but instead, all I got was sympathy.

"Have you talked to someone about this since your accident?"

"I was forced into rehab, and I attend AA meetings. I talk but I don't think it's enough." I knew I needed help, but I wasn't even sure where to begin.

"How has Tana been?" That question came out rough, almost like he hoped she had disappeared for good.

"She's been leaving me alone, surprisingly." I shrugged. "So who knows what's going on there."

"If you need help finding a reputable therapist, let me know and I can help you." Rowan pulled me closer and rested his chin on my shoulder. "Anything you need, Aiden, I'm here. And thank you for talking to me."

"If you want to end this—"

He lifted his head, his brows narrowing. "Finish that sentence."

I sighed but his threat still sent a hot shiver down my spine. "I'm serious, Rowan. I have baggage and I'm sure this isn't something you signed on for."

"So? We all have baggage. Some of our bags are just heavier to carry than others."

Rubbing the back of my neck, I tried easing some of the kink in my muscles, but it wasn't enough. It would never be enough.

"I really don't know why you want to be with me," I muttered.

"Are you trying to get me to end things with you first?"

His question surprised me because it had been something I never thought of before. Was that what I was doing? Was I trying to piss him off to the point he had enough and left me?

Rowan turned toward me, giving me his full attention. "You answered the phone. For me," he said, stabbing a finger into his chest. "Your brother, your friends, they all tried calling you tonight, but you didn't answer for them. Why would you pick up your fucking phone for me and not them and still doubt this shit between us?"

"Because you don't judge me. That's why I picked up the phone. I could probably tell you I killed someone, and you would ask if I needed help burying the body and I don't know why. What the fuck is so damn special about me?"

"Aiden." He shook his head. "Everything is special about you."

While I could hear his words, I didn't believe them.

I walked away and began pacing.

"You hardly know me, Rowan," I threw back at him, my voice raising.

"I hardly know you?" He stomped up to me and grabbed me by the collar of my shirt, spinning me back around to face him. "I know that you hate when I leave the cap off the toothpaste. I know that it drives you absolutely crazy when I don't clean out the sink after I shave but you're just as bad as me. You'll just never admit it. I also know that french fries with mustard is your favorite snack but you're self-conscious about it because you've probably been told it's a weird mix. And I *know* you're self-conscious about it because you always look around you after you add the mustard."

I huffed, shoving away from him. "Anyone could figure all of that out."

"Fine." He closed the distance between us. "That's not enough? Well, how about this? I know that you're scared. It makes sense now. You're scared to be happy because your team can't be. You blame yourself and maybe your team's families blame you too but it's not your fault. None of it is your fault. You did a job. You tried saving a little boy who was caught up in the mix and then shit went down. How the hell would you know that he was a decoy? And if you would have assumed that he was a decoy in the first place, and something happened to him because he was actually innocent? That would have fucked you up even more. You're also scared that this disease is going to take over your life more than it already has and ruin what little relationship you have left with your parents."

His words registered pain, hitting somewhere deep inside of me that had never been reached. When I went to pull out of his grasp, he pulled me closer.

"Rowan." But the strength to fight him was no longer there.

"You're scared to be happy because you feel you don't deserve it. You probably felt this way long before you were discharged from the Navy." He cupped the side of my neck, his eyes locking with mine. As much as I wanted to pull away, I found that I couldn't. "You're scared to fall in love and have a family of your own because you haven't been sure what you want. Until now. Maybe you feel like it's too late. But, Aiden, it's never too late to be happy."

My chest tightened, my breathing picking up. A cold draft washed over me, making my palms clammy.

"I…I don't know how to be happy," I confessed, my voice cracking.

"Then let me help you." Rowan leaned his forehead against mine. "Let me be what you need. Everything you need."

"I'm scared that you'll hurt me," I whispered.

"I know and I understand your fear, but I promise, baby. I promise that I will do everything in my power not to hurt you. As long as I can control it."

Grabbing his shirt, I pulled him against me and threw myself around him.

"I got you, Aiden," he whispered, returning the embrace.

I melted into his touch, needing his strength now more than ever.

Rowan leaned back, tilting his head. "Did you want to go home?"

"Yes," I croaked.

He gave me a small smile and held out his hand. "Then let's go."

(Rowan)

After finding Aiden and driving us home, we crawled into bed and watched some movies. He called his brother and reassured him that he was safe. He just had a moment and needed to be alone. But everything was fine. It was a lie. Everything wasn't fine. But I didn't correct him.

Aiden had eventually fallen asleep with his head on my lap and my fingers running through his hair.

So many truths were revealed tonight but none of them were mine. I was scared to own up to my truths. A lot of people judged when it came to being paid for sex. Aiden didn't seem to care about my past, but I couldn't help that little voice in my head that constantly nagging at me and saying it was all a lie and he did in fact judge me.

Aiden shifted beside me, pulling me from my thoughts. He was mumbling in his sleep, a sheen of sweat coating his skin.

"Shhh…" I ran my hand in circles along his upper back. "Settle, Aiden. You're fine. You're safe. It's just a nightmare."

He curled his arm around me, pushing his face into my lap and letting out a heavy sigh.

I could feel his hot breath through the thin sheet. It slid over a part of me that hadn't been given to anyone else in quite a long time. Not until him. Until the man who had been so broken, came barreling into my life like a quiet little storm.

Aiden shifted again, the sheet lowering a little down my lap at the movement. His hand cupped my hip, his thumb rubbing back and forth over the soft skin.

There had been a time where I would have taken over but with everything he had been through, I decided to see where he would take this and just how far he would go to get what he wanted. Add to the fact that I wasn't sure if he was awake or not, I was curious to see what naughty thoughts were suddenly going through his mind.

Curling his fingers into the sheet, he lifted his head and pulled the fabric off of my lap. He blew out a breath, the hot air making my cock twitch. Looked like he was awake.

"Have you ever been fucked?" he murmured.

"No." Is that what he needed? I had always been the top and the one doing the fucking but if he needed it, maybe, just maybe, I could let him fuck me instead.

Aiden wrapped his fingers around my growing shaft and licked up the length of it.

A tingle shot through me.

"What does it feel like?" he asked, closing his lips around the crown of my dick.

"*Fuck.*" I ran my fingers through his hair. "Hot. Tighter than a pussy."

"Hmmm…" He lowered his mouth down the length of my dick in one smooth move before lifting off of me. "Turn around and place your hands on the headboard."

My mouth fell open at the deep dominant tone coming from him. It was unexpected and something I thought I would never hear. Not from him.

Aiden tilted his head, raising an eyebrow. "You deaf? Do as you're fucking told."

"Geezus fuck." My dick lengthened even more, clearly liking this side of him. As much as I wanted to listen to him, a part of me wanted to see what he would do if I didn't. So I just sat there and waited.

In a quick move, Aiden grabbed hold of my cock, pulling until a shout left my lips. He lowered his hand, pumping me hard and rough.

"Fucking fuck." My eyes rolled into the back of my head, the slice of pain from his violent stroking reaching a part of me that had never been reached before.

"You're playing a dangerous game." He leaned down to my ear. "Are you sure you want to do that, Rowan?"

There was a threat hidden in his voice.

"Yes." I pushed him back, forcing his hand to release me. Before he could catch me, I jumped off the bed and rushed away from him.

I ran out of the bedroom, but I knew he would follow me. He would follow because he needed it. He needed *me*. I would give him whatever it was that he craved. I would also let him fuck me, but he would have to work for it.

"I had a threesome with my brother and a mutual friend."

I turned, finding Aiden leaning against the wall.

"But I never fucked her ass." He pushed away from the wall. "I've never been adventurous when it comes to sex but now, I know why."

"Oh? And why is that exactly, Aiden?" I backed up as he walked toward me.

"Because my fantasies, kinks, desires, whatever you want to call them, have been dormant. I didn't actually think I was into sex for the longest time but then I met you and now I want it all. You mentioned sharing someone or fucking me in front of people. The first time you stroked my dick, you had me imagining us in a room full of people with them watching."

"I did," I said, wondering what he was getting at.

He stopped coming toward me and watched me instead. "I don't want to share. I want it to be only you and me, but I'm intrigued about people watching us."

"Is that so?" I took a step toward him, taking in all of his naked glory. "You want me all to yourself, but you don't mind if others watch?"

"Yes." His gaze dropped to my cock. "Exactly."

"Do you want them to watch me fucking you or you fucking me?"

His eyes met mine at my question, a wicked grin spreading on his face.

SEVENTEEN

AIDEN

I NEEDED HIM IN ways I never knew existed.

A lot of things were still up in the air for us, and I was still dealing with my own personal demons, but one thing I did know, I *had* to fuck Rowan.

Instead of answering his question, I closed the distance between us and wrapped my hand around his throat.

He swallowed hard.

Pulling him toward me, I started walking and pushing him until his back hit the wall. Spinning him around, I kept my hand around his throat and pressed my mouth against his ear. "I need to feel it when you scream for me," I whispered, pressing my fingers into his jugular.

"*Fuck*," he muttered, placing his hands against the wall.

Kicking his legs apart, I reached around him with my free hand and began stroking his cock. Pre-cum leaked from him, sending a shiver down my spine. Swiping my fingers along the tip, I released his swollen length and dipped them between the cheeks of his ass.

His breath caught.

I grinned.

Not giving him a chance to get used to my fingers being at a part of his body he hadn't given to anyone, I shoved a finger into him.

Rowan jumped, arching against me, a low groan leaving him.

Tightening my hold on his throat, I continued fingering him. "You're tight as hell," I murmured. "Think I'll fit?"

He chuckled. "We'll make you fucking fit."

Slipping a second finger into him, I reveled in the way he arched for me. My feelings were a fucking mess. I was terrified. Even though he told me he would never leave me and that he was in this for the long run, it still didn't make me doubt him any less.

"Aiden, stop thinking and just use me."

At his words, I pulled my fingers from his body and spit into my palm. "Condom."

"No, I need to feel you," he bit out.

That confession sent a shiver down my spine. "I'm clean."

"Same, baby. I promise I'm clean too."

Lubing up my shaft, I pushed the tip between the cheeks of his ass.

With my free hand pressed against the back of his neck, I thrust into him in a rough move.

Rowan shouted, pushing back into me.

He was right. It was tight and hot. Much tighter than a pussy. Not giving either of us a chance to get used to it, I grabbed onto his hips and began fucking him.

"Aiden." My name left his lips on a whimper. "Harder. Make it fucking hurt."

A hard growl left me as I pulled him away from the wall and picked up speed with my brutal thrusts. My fingers dug into his hips, my cock ripped into him, all of my damn feelings were replaced with the need to make it so it was just me and him.

"Harder, Aiden," he demanded. "You won't hurt me."

"Fuck, I want to hurt you," I yelled, slamming my waist against his ass.

"Then do it." He pushed back against me, meeting me thrust for thrust. "Fucking hurt me."

Pulling him from the wall, I shoved him to the ground. Before he had a chance to get away, I grabbed his hips, pulled him back and shoved every inch of me into him. It forced a cry from his lips, a cry I had never heard before, not coming from him or anyone for that matter. It opened up this newfound awareness in me. This need to control. To get a hold of my life by the damn horns and fuck it up until I was better. Until everything was better.

"Yes, that's it, baby." His words of encouragement drove me forward until he was lying on the floor with me on top of him.

My hips slowed, driving into him in sensual torturous moves.

It was enough to send us both over the edge.

Both of us moaned, reveling in that simultaneous release we craved.

With my cock still seated deep in his ass, I sunk my teeth into the back of his neck.

Rowan sighed. "Fucking hell, I had no idea how much I needed that."

Was he lying? Did he actually mean what he said or was he just trying to make me feel better? I had never done this before. *Oh shit.* Maybe I hurt him. Maybe I...

I pulled out of him in a rougher move than I intended, earning me a grunt followed by a low curse.

"Sorry." I fell back on my ass, trying to get away from him but at the same time, I needed him close. I was confused. So damn confused. My thoughts were a jumbled mess. The more I tried controlling them, the messier they became. "Sorry." I curled my knees up to my chest, cupped the back of my head, and began rocking. I needed a drink. It hit me fast. That need. That desire. That damn craving.

Warm strong arms wrapped around me.

My body stiffened at first, but it only lasted a mere second before I melted into Rowan's touch.

He didn't say anything like I was sure most people would. He just held me. He didn't tell me it would be okay or that he was there for me. It was something I already knew.

Rowan pulled me into his arms, running his hand up and down my back. "Let's go take a shower," he whispered.

Those were the only words he said as he helped me up. He cupped my cheek, placing a soft peck on my mouth before pulling away.

My heart jumped as the cool air of him no longer being close, washed over me. He had disappeared into the kitchen and came back a moment later to wipe up his release off the floor.

A shiver rippled down my spine, watching him reminded me of what we had done a moment ago.

Rowan stood and came toward me. "Normally I would make you clean it up yourself. Since you are the very reason for that mess."

I swallowed hard as he neared, unable to move or look away from him.

"But I know you're going through something right now, so I'll be a gentleman." Rowan walked away, heading down the hall leading to the bathroom. "For now," he called over his shoulder.

As I followed him, I couldn't help but wonder what it would be like to live the fantasies he had put in my head. The fact that he wanted to fuck me in a room full of people intrigued me, and I had to admit, it also turned me on.

Though physically, I knew that I needed him in every single way.

Emotionally, I wasn't sure if I was ready for more or if I ever would be.

(Rowan)

Something switched between us. I wasn't sure if it was for the better or not though. Aiden lost control and my ass still burned as a result of it. But I wasn't complaining. Not in the least. Whatever he needed, I would give to him. This may be new, like he constantly reminded me, but there was something there. We needed each other whether he cared to admit it or not.

I had been going through life one fuck at a time. My sister used to constantly tell me that my dick was going to fall off.

Until I met Miguel, I had never wanted a relationship. But once I realized just how obsessive he had become, I ended that shit real fast. I never thought it would happen for me again but then Aiden came along, and everything just felt right. He brought out the possessive side of me. With the shit that Miguel had done, I had become even more protective over the broken man who was currently running his hands over my naked body.

Was I in love with him? Is this what it felt like?

"Rowan." Aiden's soft voice pulled me from my thoughts. "I'm sorry if I hurt you." His words had been so quiet beneath the sound of the running water, I wasn't sure if I had heard him correctly. "I couldn't stop myself." His eyes met mine then, his strong jaw clenching and unclenching the longer I didn't say anything.

Reaching up, I ran my fingers along the side of his cheek. "I'm falling for you, Aiden. Is it love? I have no idea. I've never been in love before. But I do feel something for you. Something that's more than friendship."

His breath caught but like a good boy, he didn't say anything.

"I don't expect you to tell me that you feel the same way, but I do know that you feel something for me. You wouldn't have fucked me the way you did if you didn't."

His cheeks turned pink, the corners of his lips twitching.

Running my fingers through his hair, I closed that final space between us until my body was pressed up against him. "I just want you know how I feel. Whether this be love, obsession, or something else, I just want you to know that I'm not going anywhere. That this is it. For me. And I hope it is for you too."

Aiden nodded but he still never said anything. Which was fine. He would tell me how he felt eventually but I wouldn't press him.

"What happened tonight?" I asked, my voice low.

He swallowed hard, his Adam's apple bobbing up and down with the movement. "I couldn't stop myself. It was like I was looking down and watching me rip into you."

"Have you ever been like that before?"

"No." Aiden ran his hands up my sides, sending tingles along with them. "I needed you in ways I can't explain. I needed to know what you felt like. I needed to hear you whimper for me. I needed you…I needed you to fucking submit to me."

And there it was.

"Why?" I tilted my head, wondering what was going on his mind.

His eyes dropped to my flaccid cock, traveling up my torso to my face. "I'm not sure exactly. My brother is the adventurous one like I told you but tonight, I needed something different. I needed you. All of you. I can't explain it." He sighed. "Now I'm rambling and repeating myself." When he went to pull away, I tugged him closer.

"Don't." Gripping his hips, I dug my fingers into the bones, asserting the dominance he craved from me.

A soft gasp escaped his full lips, his pupils dilating.

"You needed me," I murmured.

"I already told you that."

My dick jumped at the bite in his tone. "Yeah, you did but you haven't exactly told me why."

"I don't know why," he snapped.

"I think you actually do, Aiden." Grabbing hold of his cock, I tugged and pulled until he was hard from my touch.

A groan left him, his eyes fluttering closed.

Leaning forward, I nipped at his jaw. "Tell me why and I'll let you come."

"I don't know," he panted. "Fuck that feels good."

"Yes, you do know." I stroked him from base to tip, the movement slow and tortuous. He was hot, throbbing in my hand.

"Rowan," he whined, bucking his hips into my touch.

"Stop." I dug my fingers into his cock and stopped stroking. "If you want to come, you'll answer my question."

"I don't know." His eyes were dark, wild, and filled with so much damn lust, it made my own dick leak. "I really don't. I knew that I needed you. I needed to fill your hot as fuck body. I needed to own you and dominate you in any way that I could."

"Why?" I began pumping him again, the movement rough and violent.

Sounds of pleasure left him, his hips thrusting in tune with my hand. "Because."

"Because why?" I needed him to say it.

"Rowan." His breathing picked up. "Please don't stop."

"Then tell me why the fuck you needed me to submit."

"Because I needed a drink," he yelled, shoving me back.

I pushed him against the wall, dropping to my knees and taking his dick into my mouth.

Aiden shouted out my name, grabbed hold of my head, and began fucking my face. His release coated my tongue, but I wouldn't stop. He had wanted me to submit and while I was fine doing that, he was going to learn real fast who the true dominant one was between us.

"Rowan," he cried out, digging his fingers into my head. "I can't take any more."

I lapped and sucked at him, drinking up every inch of his thick cock but I wouldn't stop. Pulling my head off of him, I stroked him roughly and lowered my mouth to his balls.

"Geezus fucking fuck."

Rising to my full height, I spun him around and shoved him up against the shower wall. "You will learn real quickly that when I ask you a question, I expect an answer."

Running the tip of my cock over the tight little rim between the cheeks of his ass, I didn't let him get used to me and thrust into him.

He shouted, arching against me.

"Trying to get away, baby boy?"

"Fuck no." Aiden pushed into me, taking my dick even deeper.

"Good." Running my fingers through his hair, I ripped his head back and curled my other hand around his throat. "Then fuck yourself on my cock."

Placing his hands against the wall, he began moving his hips back and forth.

Wrapping my other hand around his throat, I squeezed just enough that he would know who owned him.

"Harder, Aiden," I demanded, my voice rough.

He whimpered, his ass probably burning since I never prepped him, but he listened and took me to the deepest part of him.

"That's it. Such a good boy." Tightening my hold on his throat, I pressed my mouth against his ear. "Who owns you, Aiden?"

"You do," he moaned.

"Whose cock is deep in your ass right now?"

"Yours," he whispered.

"Damn straight." Landing a hard swat on his rear, I leaned back. "Now be a good little boy and come."

(Aiden)

Rowan's hands were wrapped around my throat, and I was riding him. Although I was on top, with his fingers tightening on my jugular, I knew who was really in control.

I had already come twice, the evidence clear on his stomach but I couldn't stop. Even if I really wanted to, there was no way that this was ending anytime soon.

"That's it, baby. Fuck." Rowan groaned. "You take my cock like such a good boy."

His words of praise sent a hot shiver down my spine. I had never been one who needed to be praised or coddled before, but coming from someone like him, I found that it only turned me on. It also satisfied a part of me that hadn't seen the light of day in years. I couldn't quite explain it, but it was like because I felt I was a disappointment to my family and friends, Rowan praising me eased some of that anxiety.

With my hands on his chest, I moved my hips and back and forth.

"Yes, just like that." His breathing picked up. "Faster."

I did as I was told, undulating my hips against him.

"Fuck, Aiden." His hands squeezed tighter around my throat, my air being cut off just enough that I gasped.

His dick pulsed inside of me, forcing a moan from my mouth.

When he calmed down, he released me and helped me off of him.

Lying on my stomach, I sighed, letting the events of the night wash over me.

Rowan slipped from the bed and came back a few minutes later. "You good?" he asked, running something warm between the cheeks of my ass.

"Yeah," I whispered.

"You sure?" He kissed my shoulder. "Do you want more?"

"I don't know if I can handle more," I confessed.

"That wasn't my question." Rowan rolled me onto my back, staring down at me. "Answer me."

"Yes." I ran my fingers along the dark scruff on his strong jaw. "I want more."

He smirked. "Good boy."

EIGHTEEN

AIDEN

It had been just over a week since that night. Maybe even longer. Both Rowan and I used each other in very different ways. When I had told him I wanted him to submit, I was shocked at my own confession. While I found that I actually enjoyed being the top, submitting to him was what I wanted most. No. It was what I *needed*. I just didn't know it until I practically ripped him apart.

We had been spending every second we could together. I enjoyed being with him but a part of me still feared that he would get sick of me. That he would up and leave and tell me that I had too much baggage for him or that he couldn't do it anymore. That he would give up on me like my own father had. It was unfair of me to think that when I had put both him and Mom through so much, but I couldn't help it. Especially whenever I saw them, and he looked at me with disdain.

I still attended AA meetings, but I also hadn't had a single drop of alcohol either. Did I even need to go to these meetings? Would they help me? They were mostly depressing. I never shared my story. Rowan had been the first person I told every single thing about that dreaded time in the Navy. I had told my brother some of my truths but not all. I loved him but he judged. I never blamed him though.

"Aiden."

My head snapped up at my name, finding Vince Junior coming toward me. He was the youngest of us kids and happened to be married to the oldest. I had no idea how he convinced Gigi's father to let that go down, but he did.

"How's it going, Vince?" I asked, leaning a hip against the table that held blueprints of what we were supposed to be working on. But I couldn't focus. Especially not with the way Rowan had left things that morning.

"Don't come," Rowan whispered in my ear. "You're going to think of me all damn day and wonder when I'll give you that release you crave. It'll happen. I'm just not going to tell you when." As soon as those words left his lips, he took my cock to the back of his throat and swallowed every inch of me. He got me so worked up that I began fucking his face, which earned me a deep chuckle in return. But he still never let me come.

I had been semi-hard ever since. He texted me every hour or so, checking in to make sure I hadn't touched myself. I hadn't. Because I needed to listen to him. I needed his praise and for him to be proud of me.

"Not too bad." Vince came up beside me, picking up the blueprint. "You?"

"I'm alright. How's the family?" I quickly asked before he could question me. Truth was, I wasn't alright. But no one needed to know that. No one but Rowan and possibly my parents, if they ever talked to me again.

"They are good. Really good. The kids are keeping me on my toes and the wife?" Vince winked. "Well, we both know how that's going."

I chuckled and for the first time, the laughter didn't feel forced. Not like before. "You're good for each other."

"We try to be." Vince went on to talk about his family and ended up with him showing me pictures of his kids. While he spoke, I tried listening, I tried soaking up information from a friend I had known for years. But when he just looked at me, a frown forming between his brows, I knew he had asked me something and I never responded like I was supposed to.

"I'm sorry." I cleared my throat, my cheeks heating. I didn't like this. This vulnerability rushing through me. Rowan had been the only one who had ever seen it and he took care of me after. But this…this felt way too personal.

"It's okay, Aiden," Vince said gently. "I know I'm much younger than you, but I do consider you a friend. If you ever need anything, please don't hesitate to call me."

Before I could respond, he walked away, taking the blueprint with him, and started barking orders at some of the guys we worked with.

I sighed, running a hand through my hair.

My phone took that moment to vibrate in my back pocket. Fishing it out, I saw a text from Rowan.

Rowan: I'm going to be late tonight, but I'll bring home food for us.

Me: Okay.

Rowan: You good?

Me: Now I am.

Rowan: Good.

I could almost hear his assertive tone from here.

Putting my phone away, I finished up my work and ducked out before anyone noticed. The guys had been used to me being quiet lately. Guess it helped that I was also one of the owners but really, Ashton was more of an owner than I was. The guys also felt the same. They never came to me for direction, going to my brother instead. Couldn't say I blamed them really. I had been less than dependable ever since I had been discharged from the Navy. It felt like so damn long ago, it was almost like it had been nothing but a nightmare.

After changing out of my work boots to my running shoes, I put everything away in the office I shared with Ashton.

Leaving the yard we had been building the house on, I shoved my hands into my pockets and walked. I didn't want to go home just yet. I wasn't sure where I was going exactly but I knew I just needed to keep moving.

Picking up the pace, my leg muscles began to burn. It had been a long time since I worked out. Thankfully working in construction helped keep me active enough, it was like I still lifted weights. But it wasn't enough. Something tugged inside of me, pulling at my soul. It was trying to tell me something. To warn me maybe. I wasn't sure. A part of me was scared. Should I run toward it? Should I run away? A thought came to me. I should run *with* it.

Before I knew what I was doing, I was running. My arms pumped at my sides as I tried going faster and faster. Once my heart damn near pounded out of my chest, I slowed to a steady pace but didn't stop.

I had never been a runner but anytime was a good time to start.

My lungs burned, my legs ached, but it felt so fucking good. I embraced the pain.

Doing a mental scan of my body, I realized that I enjoyed this feeling. Sweat started dripping down my face, my shirt clung to my torso, the soles of my feet were on fire since I was wearing old running shoes. But this...this was what I needed. Not alcohol. Not even sex. Although that was delicious.

Running.

That was what I needed.

It was my therapy.

The next thing I knew, I was in front of my parents' place. I stopped at the end of the sidewalk that led up the long path to the large backsplit.

Taking deep breaths, I slowed my racing heart and wiped my face with the end of my shirt. Checking my phone, I realized that

I had been running for almost an hour. No wonder every inch of me hurt.

I wasn't sure what I was doing here but obviously something called me to it for a reason. I hadn't talked to my parents in a while. The last time ended up in a fight I didn't want to relive. So, I stayed away. Then I ended up in an accident and I saw my parents age ten years before my eyes. I put them through a lot and even though I could never tell them how sorry I was for the stress I caused, they were just words, it wouldn't make a difference.

Once I was standing on the front porch, I took a deep breath and knocked on the door. It slowly swung open a moment later, revealing my mom.

"Aiden." Her eyes widened. "What are you doing here? And why are you knocking? Don't you have your key still?"

"I'm sorry." I coughed, not really planning for this. I still had my key but I never kept it on me since I felt like a stranger around my family and friends most days. "Is this a bad time?"

"No." She shook her head, her shoulder-length curls bouncing with the movement. "Not at all. This will always be your home." She stepped aside, letting me enter the familiar space. "Your dad's just in the shower but he should be out soon."

"Okay." I stood there, leaned against the wall, and waited because I wasn't sure what to do. Sure, this had been my home, once, but now I felt out of place. I hadn't felt welcome for a long time. Maybe even before I joined the Navy. When that realization dawned on me, my eyes widened a bit.

"What's wrong?" Mom asked, lightly touching my arm.

"I'm sorry. For everything. I know I've put you through a lot and I'll never forgive myself for it, but I am…I am so sorry." My voice cracked, my eyes welling as the words left me.

"Oh." Mom's chin wobbled. "God, I've missed you." She threw herself around my middle, squeezing me with everything in her.

"I've missed you too," I whispered, hugging her back. For the first time in a very long time, I longed for her motherly touch. I had thought for years that I could handle this shit on my own but since meeting Rowan, I realized I couldn't and that I needed help carrying this added weight on my shoulders.

"Aiden."

I jumped, finding my dad standing at the entrance to the hall.

He looked shocked to see me, much like my mom did at first, but at the same time, he also looked pissed. His jaw clenched and unclenched, his body stiff like he was waiting for a fight. He wouldn't get one though. Not from me. Not anymore.

"I'm sorry for just showing up like this," I said, my voice small.

"You do not need to apologize." Mom cupped my cheek, her eyes moving back and forth over my face. "Did you work out?"

"I went for a run and showed up here." I looked down at myself. "I should have changed first."

"Don't worry about it." She gave me a small smile. "I'm sure some of your clothes that are here will still fit. Why don't you go shower and change?"

I looked at Dad then, waiting for him to say something but when he didn't and only stared at me instead, I nodded.

"Did you want to stay for supper?" Mom asked. "We would love it if you did. Wouldn't we, Asher?"

Dad crossed his arms under his broad chest. "Sure."

"Okay," I murmured and like a puppy with his tale between his legs, I left them in the hall and went up to the set of stairs that would lead to the second floor. When I looked back at my parents, Dad was watching me. He was probably wondering what the hell I was doing. If I knew, I would tell him. But for now, I would take this one second at a time because it was all I could do.

(Rowan)

I was worried about Aiden. It was to the point my stomach hurt and thinking about him made my chest ache. My thoughts were consumed by him. Every single thing that made up Aiden Donovan took over my damn life.

The last text I got from him was an hour ago and, while he told me he was good, I knew for a fact he wasn't.

I spent all day researching PTSD and how the BDSM lifestyle could be good for people who suffered from this illness. And how it could help people with alcoholism as well. It got to the point that my brain started to hurt, and I was going cross-eyed from all the reading I had done. Between that and helping customers buy whatever it was they wanted to from my antique shop, I was mentally done.

Add to the fact that Miguel had texted several times throughout the day and even called a handful of times as well, I just wanted to wrap myself up in Aiden and disappear.

When I had told him not to touch himself after I wouldn't let him come that morning, I wondered if he listened to me. I had a feeling that he did. While he wasn't truly submissive, he *needed* to listen to me. Sure, I loved switching for him and feeling him overpower me, but it was him bottoming for me that truly got us both hard as fuck.

Me: You still hard, baby boy?

Aiden: For you? Always.

My dick twitched.

Dropping my phone on top of my desk, I let out a harsh sigh and scrubbed my hands up and down my face a couple of times. Slapping my cheeks to try and wake myself up a bit to get some actual work done, I gave myself a shake as well.

Attempting to make a living the legal way was harder than one would think. Especially when I was used to a certain lifestyle. Not that I lived in a fancy apartment or anything, nor did I really didn't flaunt my money around. But I had set some cash aside for my nephews for school once they were old enough. I also set enough aside for my parents so they could retire. My mom would question where I got the money from but I knew my dad wouldn't even bat an eye. Neither of them could really say anything though, seeing as both of them used to do the same when they were my age.

But trying to change careers when people expected certain things from you was a pain in the ass to say the least.

I had to be careful how I let my clients know that I was retiring as well. I didn't need them coming after me or my family. But the one I was truly worried about was Miguel. He was unwell and it made me nervous.

Since I wasn't able to concentrate much, I closed up my computer and decided to call it a night. Then Aiden texted that he needed picking up. It had been on the tip of my tongue to tell him that he should start going to meetings again. It had been selfish on my part when it seemed like he wanted to use me instead to help himself feel better. It had been a long time since I had this much sex. The past week had been work, fuck, eat, sleep, fuck some more, and not all in that order either.

Together, we opened a door into Aiden's fantasies. Fantasies he never even knew he had. Until me.

I had a goal in mind. Besides making him fall in love with me, I had a goal to make him submit in ways he never knew existed. From toys to playrooms and more, we would explore every delicious desire he had and learn together.

NINETEEN

AIDEN

ONCE I WAS DONE my shower, I quickly got changed. I didn't want to overstay my welcome. Although I knew that my mom would be fine if I spent hours here or even stayed the night, it was my dad that I was more worried about. He wasn't happy that I had shown up unannounced. Especially when I hadn't really talked to him since my accident. And that had been months ago.

Before I left my room, I took a look around. My mom had left it the same. Ashton and I had shared a room for years until we got older. And then eventually our parents made it so we could have our own separate rooms. Although the house wasn't overly big, Dad had built a room in the basement for Ashton, while I had a room upstairs. My mom had worried that we would fight because who wouldn't want their room in the basement?

But I didn't really care about that.

I spent years trying to separate myself from Ashton. We were fraternal twins, but still looked very much alike, and as we got older, people could tell us apart. But at first glance, we were often mistaken for each other.

Now that we had gotten older, I had lost a lot of weight. Alcohol was the noose around my neck and if I wasn't careful, it would destroy me. I knew that if I didn't get my life back on track, it would eventually kill me. Or I would kill someone else. I voiced my truths to Rowan, but I hadn't told him everything. I hadn't told him how I felt and how I could feel the alcohol tightening its hold on my neck or that it was a feeling I craved. I submitted to it. Much like I submitted to him. While, it was different with Rowan, it was also the same as well.

As I looked around my room, I noticed for the first time how it was much like my personality. I constantly changed the furniture around. As a teen, I would put new posters on the wall every few months. Seeing the posters of the different bands I had grown up loving, brought me back to a fight I had with my dad. It seemed that even before I became an alcoholic, I fought with him often. Mom had said it was because we were so much alike that we butted heads, but I wasn't sure if that was the case. I never had the courage to ask him.

A part of me felt like he didn't like me much.

I knew he loved me because it was his job to love me. But anything more than that, I wasn't so sure.

Was he even proud of me?

"Yes, I'm proud of you."

I spun around, not expecting my dad to be standing at the doorway. I didn't realize I had spoken out loud. The question hung between us even though he had given me an answer.

It wasn't enough.

"Why are you proud of me?" I blurted.

"You joined the Navy and followed in my footsteps."

I scoffed. "Yeah, and I ended up becoming an alcoholic as well."

"I know." He paused. "I'm sorry."

My mouth fell open. It took a second for his words to register. "Why are *you* sorry?" I finally asked him.

"I feel like I pushed you too hard. Ashton was the smart one because he didn't listen to me." Dad shoved his hands into the pockets of his jeans, shifting from side to side. He was uncomfortable. I could feel the struggle within him because I felt it on a day-to-day basis.

"Do you regret pushing me to join the Navy?"

"A part of me does. I often wonder if you hadn't joined the Navy, would you be an alcoholic now?"

"I've wondered the same thing, but I've always had an addictive personality, so I think no matter what, it would have happened eventually." Once I found something I liked, even in my younger years, I became obsessed with it and wouldn't stop until it took over my life. "I think what happened just triggered it."

"I don't know what happened, Aiden."

"Stuff." It was a lame answer, but it was the only one I could think of at the moment.

"Stuff. Stuff happened." Dad's jaw clenched and I knew that this was about to turn into a fight. I hadn't seen them in a while, and I didn't want this visit to be like that.

I had every intention of also telling them about Rowan. They knew I had moved in with someone after I found an ad because Ashton told them, but I needed to tell them I was sleeping with my roommate. Maybe not in those words, but I definitely needed to tell them I was in a relationship with a guy.

Would they judge me?

Did they already know?

It was on the tip of my tongue to tell my dad everything. From what happened in the Navy to what I was doing now.

"I'm scared," I said instead.

Dad came farther into the room, looked around, and ended up sitting on the double bed. He patted the spot beside him.

I sat, wringing my hands together in my lap.

"I don't want to fight," Dad muttered.

"I don't want to fight either, but I feel like it's all I know how to do anymore with you."

"I know." Dad sighed, running a hand through his graying hair. "I feel the same way."

"I'm seeing someone." I figured there was no point in keeping it to myself any longer, so I just came out and said it. "I'm also happy. The happiest I've been in a while. Actually, I think it's the happiest I've ever been in my whole entire life. I still have…problems but he's helping me through them. He's patient as hell." I laughed lightly to myself. "Maybe too patient." I shook my head, clearing my throat. "I know I've never hinted at being interested in guys before. I guess I was never interested in women either. Rowan is good for me."

When Dad didn't say anything, I looked at him and much to my surprise, he had a huge smile on his face.

"Why are you smiling?"

"Because you're happy," his voice cracked.

"Really?"

"Of course." The smile fell from his face. "You think I don't want you to be happy?"

"Well, I don't know anymore. It's not like we talk much. And if we do talk, it usually ends with us fighting. And then Mom ends up being the referee between us. That's why I've stayed away."

"I'm sorry. I should have reached out to you."

"No, I'm sorry. I could have reached out to you instead. But I'm scared. I'm scared that all of you think I'm going to relapse again, but I haven't had a drink. Not since my accident. I swear I haven't."

"I believe you, Aiden." Dad covered my hands that were resting on my lap. "I just want you happy. That's it. That's all we both want. But I didn't know how to come out and ask you if you're happy."

"Really? You're not mad?" Having different sexual preferences other than just being straight, gay or bisexual, was normal now but I still wasn't sure how my parents would react to their son dating someone of the same sex.

Dad's frown deepened. "Why would I be mad? You're happy, aren't you?"

"Yes, I am happy."

"Then that's all that matters. There's no reason for me to be mad."

"But I mean, I'm with a guy. The same sex as me."

"So? You do realize that your mom and I don't really care what you're into as long as you're safe and happy."

"I don't know what to say. I've never really been into sex or anything. And I know that you know that I'm not a virgin. But ever since I met Rowan, I realized what I was missing. I know most people or a lot of people, anyway, come out when they're younger. But I guess I didn't realize what I wanted." I took a deep breath, massaging the back of my neck to try and ease some of the anxiety suddenly rushing through me. "I don't know what I'm trying to say."

"I get it, Aiden. I do. It took me a long time to realize that your mom was who I was supposed to be with. I tried fighting my feelings for her because I didn't think I was good enough. But she made me realize that I *am* good enough. We've tried instilling that in you boys. We just want you happy. That's all we've ever wanted. And I'm sorry for pushing you to join the Navy. I'm sorry that you felt like you couldn't come to me. I'm sorry that we fought this whole time," his voice became thick with emotion. "Your mom said it's because you and I are a lot alike. We're both pigheaded and stubborn. But I'm sorry. I am. For everything." Dad squeezed my hands harder, tightening his hold on me.

My eyes welled. My throat closing in on itself. "I just…I wish we could go back in time. I wish I'd never joined the Navy. I wish I never saw…" A shuttered breath left me.

"Did you want to talk about it?" Dad asked gently.

I didn't, but I knew that I had to tell him. I needed him to understand. I just needed him. I needed my dad. So, I told him everything. From the kid I saw who I thought was in danger to it being a setup and my squad dying as a result of it. Once the truth came out, Dad wrapped his arm around my shoulders. My body shook with silent cries. Although I still had to work through my disease and find myself a new sponsor, telling my father what happened helped lift a heavy weight from my shoulders. A weight that had been there for a long time.

"Thank you."

I wiped under my eyes looking up at my dad. "For what?"

"For talking to me. For telling me what happened. But I can't say this enough. I *am* sorry."

"I'm sorry too." A thought came to me. "How do you think Mom will react?" I asked, needing to change the subject.

"I think your mom will react just fine." Dad gave me a small smile. "Have you told Ashton?"

"No, but he did ask me a while ago if I'm gay. And I told him no, because I'm not and he told me that he didn't care either. He also said he just wanted me happy."

"That's what all of us want, Aiden."

"I know."

"Did you want me to get your mom?"

"Yes. Please." I knew I had to tell her and it would look better coming from me.

Dad rose from the bed and went to the door. "Meeka, can you come here for a moment please?"

Once Mom joined him at the door, Dad kissed her cheek and looked back at me. "Aiden has something he would like to talk to you about."

TWENTY

ROWAN

IT HAD BEEN A few days since Aiden came out to his parents and told them that we were dating. Seeing each other? Fucking. Yeah, definitely that.

He told me that his dad had been fantastic about it and his mom, even better. She started crying and told him how proud she was of him. Aiden had gotten choked up about it when he told me and I couldn't be happier for him. My parents had been just as good about me not only being into women.

Aiden's attitude seemed to shift a bit ever since he went over to his parents' place. He was happier and had a bounce in his step. He also couldn't stop smiling, which in turn, made me smile just the same. As cliché as it sounded, his smile lit up his whole face. He had put on some weight as well and made plans to start running regularly. I was proud of him. His disease would be something he would deal with for the rest of his life but no matter what, I would be there for him and now that he had talked to his parents, they could start making amends.

We were now on our way to my parents' place. I had hoped that they could help him with his issue over this current sponsor but even if they couldn't, I really wanted them to meet the guy I was falling for.

"What will I say that we are if they ask?" Aiden ran a finger along my jaw. "I can't tell them that we're fucking. That would be rude."

"You can tell them that we're friends. With a little more." And hopefully everything else eventually. I didn't want to add any pressure on him though, when he had already been through so much and was dealing with baggage I hoped one day he would let me help carry. For now, I was going to introduce him to my parents and see if they could help him with getting a new sponsor or at least point him in the right direction.

He nodded. "Okay, I like that."

Locking up the apartment, I tried not to watch Aiden. Even though things seemed to be moving in the right direction between him and his parents, he was still a flight risk. So, it was hard not to keep an eye on him.

"We can take my car," I told him.

"Good, because I…uh…I can't drive," he mumbled that confession, his cheeks turning pink. "I got a DUI and haven't been behind a wheel since."

"You never told me that." When we reached the elevator doors, I found Aiden looking at me with an odd expression on his face. "What?"

"You don't judge me?"

"Trust me." I scoffed. "I've done a lot of shitty things in my life. I was raised well. My parents are fucking amazing. But I get bored easily and have tested…boundaries in a way." In all honesty, I just took over my parents' role as providing people with information. I was the one who forced them into retirement when they realized I could do what they could with a computer and more. I would get random lectures about it from my mom, but it only went so far, when she realized, as cliché as it sounded, that the apple didn't fall far from the tree. "I do wish you would have told me about the DUI though." Was that really my issue?

"I'm used to people judging." Aiden ran a hand through his hair. "That's why I never said anything."

I stopped, turning around to face him. "Have I ever judged you? This whole time we've been together, have I ever once given you any reason to think that I was judging you?"

Aiden swallowed hard, shaking his head. "No, you haven't but to be fair, we usually just walk everywhere. I never thought to tell you that I don't have a car and that I'm not allowed to drive."

I stared at him, wondering what my deal was. He had told me he had gotten into an accident and was forced into rehab. I should have put two and two together that he would have lost his license. Why the hell was I picking a fight with him?

Blowing out a slow breath, I mentally counted to ten before closing the distance between us. "I'm sorry." I cupped the back of his neck and pulled him closer.

"For what?" he asked, licking his bottom lip.

"I think I'm just nervous about you meeting my parents and I know you still have some walls up. I don't blame you. Please don't think that I do but I guess it's getting to me a bit." That was the truth and I hoped that one day, even if it was years from now, he would eventually give me all of him.

"I want to open myself up to you," he murmured. "But I need you to be patient with me."

I placed a soft peck on his mouth. "I will try and do that."

When the doors dinged open, I pulled away from him and stepped into the elevator with Aiden following behind me. "You will never receive any judgement from me. I can even drive you to your meetings if you want."

"I usually just walk but thank you. I'll consider that. Especially if it's raining. But walking helps clear my head."

"That's why I run." I leaned against the wall. "I know you just started running but you can join me. I run four days a week. When you feel up to it of course. But there are other ways that I'd rather get my cardio in." I waggled my eyebrows, trying to lighten the mood.

Aiden slipped into the corner of the elevator, shoving his hands in the front pockets of his jeans, pulled them out and slid them back into the pockets. He repeated the movements a couple of times, his eyes moving back and forth. He blew out slow, even breaths.

"Is it the elevator?" I asked, tilting my head. He must not have heard my innuendo. Any other time and he would have commented about it but now, he was nervous and I didn't like it.

"I don't know," he whispered.

I hit a button that would make the elevator stop on the next floor. Even though we only had three floors to go, I didn't need him having a panic attack.

"Come," I told him as soon as the doors opened.

He rushed past me, letting out a heavy sigh once we were out in the hall.

"Better?" I asked him, wanting to pull him into my arms and comfort him but thought it would be best if he came to me first.

"Yeah." He gave himself a shake. "Thank you."

I only nodded and made my way down the hall. "We can take the stairs."

He fell in step beside me, his shoulder brushing mine.

My head lifted, my eyes landing on his face.

His gaze flicked to mine. "How did you know?"

"My dad gets panic attacks every now and again. My mom said that it's from PTSD, but my sister and I don't know the details as to why. They don't talk about it. Something bad happened in his childhood. That's all we know. But when my mom isn't around to help him, my sister and I have to step in sometimes. It's not often that our parents aren't together though."

"My parents have tried helping me and even my brother has, but I usually just drink away the panic attacks. I know that doesn't sound good but it's the truth." Aiden was stiff beside me, his hands shoved in the front pockets of his jeans.

"I get it. I've never had a panic attack, but I understand and have seen firsthand how awful they are."

He only grunted and never responded.

"I feel like we should have talked about this weeks ago," I said, pointing out the obvious.

"We've taken the elevator before, and I've been fine. The panic attacks don't always happen, but I can't control them. They can come on at any time," he explained. "Besides…we started fucking and everything else was shoved aside."

His words grated on my last nerve.

When we reached the main floor of the apartment building and headed out into the early morning air, I grabbed Aiden's arm and shoved him up against the wall.

His breath caught, his pupils dilating at the rough move.

"We took so many steps forward and now it's like we're taking hundreds back." I pushed my waist into him, reveling in the way his cock twitched against mine. "This…right here…is home. You got me, Aiden? No more keeping shit to yourself. Even if you want to just fight, fuck, fuck while fighting, talking while fucking, I don't give a shit, but I promise that if you don't start opening up to me, even if it's little bits at a time, I will make it so you walk funny for the rest of your fucking life."

"Promise?" he threw at me, his mouth pulling up into a mischievous grin.

"You drive me fucking crazy."

"Good." Aiden grabbed the back of my head and pulled me forward until our mouths crashed together. He shoved his tongue between my lips, controlling the kiss until he forced a moan from the back of my throat.

Before this could turn into anything more, I released him, leaning my forehead against his.

"I'm sorry," he whispered, brushing his fingers along my mouth.

"We'll get through this, Aiden. I'm not going anywhere and if you don't know by now, I'm stubborn as fuck."

"Thank you, Rowan." He slipped out from between me and the wall. "Let's go introduce me to your parents."

(Aiden)

Never before had I ever met the parents of someone I was dating or sleeping with, so this was all new for me.

Even though I had talked to my own parents, and we seemed to be on the mend, I still couldn't help but wonder if it would eventually backfire. I also couldn't help but think back to one of the last fights I had with my dad.

"The next time you show up here, drunk off your ass, will be the least of your concern." Dad had me by the collar of my shirt. He faded in and out in front of me. It was on the tip of my tongue to dare him to hit me.

His face reddened, the scowl deepening on his face.

Maybe I had actually said those words out loud. Oops.

"I don't even know who you are anymore." He shoved me back so damn hard I tripped over my feet and fell against the wall. *"You push your mom again and I'll fucking kill you. I don't give a shit anymore that you're my son."*

Please don't give up on me.

I need help.

Help me.

Those words were silent in my mind as I tried begging him to be there. To be there for me. But I didn't deserve it. He was right. I couldn't stop it. The demons were too loud. The images of what had happened were there. Constantly. They laughed in my face, egging me on. It was like they were challenging me and seeing just how far they could actually push me before I snapped and lost it completely.

"Aiden?"

I jumped, my head spinning around. Rowan was looking at me with a deep frown set between his eyebrows.

"Sorry," I mumbled, my cheeks heating.

"You good?" he asked, looking back out at the road ahead of us.

"Yeah, I am. Maybe not one-hundred-percent but definitely better than before." I cupped his hand that was resting on my inner thigh, brushing my thumb along the side of his wrist. I leaned my head back against the seat, wondering how his parents were going to react to meeting me.

"Do you think your parents will like me?" I asked him, needing the sounds of our voices to drown out the noise in my head.

"Yes, I do. We should be there soon. They actually live just outside the city in a small bungalow. We didn't have a lot growing up, but my parents made sure to fill our home with warmth and love. It sounds cheesy but knowing what some kids go through, I will never complain."

I turned my head, looking at him then. "We had a good childhood too."

"My sister lucked out and married a good guy as well."

"My brother married a good woman."

"Do you want to get married one day, Aiden?" Rowan asked, his voice lowering an octave.

"I never really thought about it until I met you."

Rowan glanced at me, a cheeky grin spreading on his face.

"I mean…" I laughed. "No, that's exactly what I mean. I'm not proposing or anything but I like this and I like seeing where it's going to go."

"I know how you feel," Rowan said, blowing out a slow breath, inching his hand higher up my thigh.

He ended up changing the subject and we started talking about our favorite movies, the types of music we liked to listen to, and anything else that could take our mind off the heavy subject matter. While marriage had never been discussed, it was definitely a nice thought. I could see myself falling for him one day. Maybe I already had. He had helped me through so much already. I really couldn't thank him enough.

TWENTY-ONE

ROWAN

"I DON'T THINK I'VE ever been to this part of the city," Aiden said, leaning forward.

"My parents own a tattoo parlor downtown and used to live above it but since they had my sister and me, they decided to buy a house and just keep the apartment as a spare. But I tease them and tell them it's their fuck pad." I chuckled, remembering how my mom blushed when I suggested it.

"Gotta get away from the kids sometimes." Aiden laughed.

I glanced at him and winked. "Exactly."

"I hope now that I talked to my parents, we can become close again." He cupped my hand that was still resting on his inner thigh.

"You will," I told him, linking our fingers. "I have a confession," I added after a beat of silence.

"What's that?" he asked, looking at me then.

"I never liked being touched or had ever wanted to be touched, and then you come along and I…" I lifted our joined hands. "I like this. I like you. I like what we've done."

"You mean that you like that we fucked." He smirked, bringing our joined hands up to his mouth and placing a soft peck on my inner wrist.

"Well, that's just an added bonus but keep looking at me like that and we'll never make it to my parents' place." I only chuckled when his cheeks turned pink.

We drove the rest of the way in a comfortable silence. A new feeling washed over me. It was a feeling I thought I felt a while ago, but I hadn't been sure. Not until now. Not until Aiden trusted that I would help him. I could sense a wall cracking between us. It had been one I wanted to break down for a while. But maybe it had been my own wall. I hadn't heard from Miguel recently and I didn't know why. When I wasn't worrying about him and what he would do, I was able to become closer to Aiden and because of that, I was falling in love with him. It was the only thing that made sense. It forced a smile to my lips, a sense of peace washing over me. Now I just needed to figure out when the right time to tell him would be.

"We're almost there," I told Aiden, releasing his hand and pointing to a house far off in the distance. "My dad wanted to take my mom and move her to a small island. He said he was kidding but a part of me wonders."

"An island is probably safer sometimes." Aiden shifted in his seat. He was fidgety and wouldn't stop moving.

"Ain't that the fucking truth." I pulled the car down a long driveway. Even though my parents lived in the city technically, my dad was able to find a house in a more remote location. I never understood why as a kid but now that I was older, I definitely got it.

"I'm nervous." Aiden ran his hands up and down his thighs. "Really nervous all of a sudden."

"Don't be. My dad's a big fucker but he's a teddy bear. Just ask my mom." Although, she would be the only one who could get away with actually referring to him as such.

Once I pulled the car into their long driveway, I parked far enough away that we would have to walk for a few minutes to give Aiden some time to calm his nerves. Killing the engine, I turned to him. "I'm not forcing anything on you, but my parents could help you and hopefully give you some advice when it comes to this Tana chick." Just saying her name made me want to cut someone.

Aiden glanced at me, a slow grin spreading on his face. "You're jealous."

"I'm not jealous." I rolled my eyes.

"Yes." He grabbed my hand and placed it on his lap. "You are."

"This is mine." I pushed my palm against him, his cock lengthening under my touch.

"It is." Aiden ran his hand up my forearm. "So, you have nothing to worry about. Besides, Tana hasn't tried contacting me lately. I think she moved on to someone else."

"I've heard that you can go through a few different sponsors before finding the right one. But I swear to God, if you get another woman who wants nothing but sex, I'll burn the fucking world down."

Aiden scoffed, rolling his eyes that time. "I don't think that'll ever happen."

Before I could say any more on it, movement caught the corner of my eye. My mom had stepped out onto the porch with a cup of coffee between her hands. Even though I couldn't see her well from where I was sitting, I knew it was coffee she was drinking because besides water, that was her only vice.

She gave us a small wave and sat on the patio couch.

"My parents can help," I told Aiden, not looking his way. "If they can't I will, but I meant what I said, Aiden." I reached for the back of his neck and pulled him closer. "I'll burn the fucking world down. All of it. So, you better remember who you belong to."

(Aiden)

Rowan's words forced the nerves away and replaced them with a need to call him out on his bluff. Not that I ever would but I did have to wonder exactly what he would do if another woman hit on me.

"Whenever you're ready, Aiden," Rowan said, leaning his head into the car. "No rush. At all."

Instead of responding, I left the vehicle. Knowing I should just get this done and over with, I slammed the door closed and went around the car, then I was standing beside a guy who had been placed in my life for a reason.

"Whatever you think is going to happen, probably won't. My parents are good people. They don't judge and they raised us not to either." Rowan tilted his head, his eyes locking with mine. "But if you want to leave, just say the word and we can go. You won't get any issues from me. I promise."

"No." I stepped closer, hooking my pinky around his. "Let's do this."

He nodded, placing a soft peck on my cheek. "I got you, baby," he whispered, leading the way up to his parents' place. His mom must have gone back into the house because I didn't see her sitting on the patio couch anymore.

"Anything I should know ahead of time?" I asked but before he could respond, the front door opened again, revealing a large man. He wore an eye patch and was heavily tattooed. While he looked lethal as fuck, when he saw at his son, his good eye warmed.

"Hey, Son." He stepped away, letting us walk by him and into the house. "We weren't expecting you."

"I know. This was kind of last minute." Rowan nodded toward me. "Dad, this is Aiden. Aiden, this is my dad, Lucas."

"It's nice to meet you," I told him, sticking out my hand because it was the polite thing to do when really, I wanted to hide in a corner somewhere with a bottle of anything. I didn't have a preference but fuck me, I could use a drink. The thought struck me hard, almost knocking me off my feet. It had been a while since I craved that vice. The only vice that would kill me. Rowan had kept me distracted enough that I never thought of reaching for a bottle. I knew I had a lot of work cut out for me, but I wasn't expecting this craving to come on so strong.

Lucas stuck his hand in mine, returning the handshake. His good eye locked on me, staring a little too long. "You look familiar."

My back stiffened. "I do?" I asked, pulling my hand from his.

"You do." His head turned as his wife joined us.

"I'm Lily." She smiled and I instantly felt better. "He does look familiar, I agree there."

"See?" Lucas wrapped an arm around her shoulders. "I'm not losing it."

"Yet," Rowan added.

"Let's get out of the doorway and head to the back," Lily suggested.

Walking through the house, I followed them to the backyard but stuck close to Rowan. He stopped, and I almost bumped into him. He turned, raising an eyebrow.

"Sorry," I muttered.

"Don't be." Something flashed in his eyes. "You good? You looked far away there when you were shaking my dad's hand."

"I wanted a drink," I confessed. "I know I'll always want a drink, but the craving was strong. You've helped kept my mind off of it, so I wasn't expecting it."

"I imagine you won't believe me, but you do have this, Aiden. And you will get through this. But just remember, you have to do this for you. You can't do it for anyone else. Not your parents, your friends, your brother. Not even for me." Rowan gently stabbed a finger against my chest. "You have to do it for you."

"I know." I blew out a slow breath. "I do know that."

A throat clearing pulled us away from each other.

"Did you want a glass of lemonade?" Lily asked, looking between us.

"Sure, please." I would prefer something harder but these people who I didn't know, didn't need to be bothered by my problems.

"So, Rowan, what brings you both by?" Lucas asked, sitting on the patio couch.

"Aiden is having an issue with his…" Rowan glanced my way.

I nodded, giving him the encouragement to continue.

"Sponsor," Rowan finished.

"Oh?" Lucas sat forward.

Lily paused in pouring the drinks, looking my way. "You're my son's roommate now."

I swallowed hard. "I don't mean any trouble. I just…"

"Trust me, sweetheart." She laughed. "I would never think that. Lord knows that Lucas and I have our own share of…trouble. I just want to get to know Rowan's new…" She looked at Rowan quickly before back to me. "Friend."

"Subtle, Mom." Rowan rolled his eyes.

"What?" She handed him a glass of lemonade before turning to me and handing me one as well. "What problem are you having?"

"I think my sponsor wants to sleep with me and not actually help me with my drinking…" My throat went dry. "Issue."

Lucas muttered a curse. "I can't tell you how many issues I had in the beginning trying to get a sponsor myself."

"Really?" Lily looked at her husband. "You never told me that."

"It was a long time before you came around and saved my life, Lilypad," he told her.

She sat down beside Lucas and grabbed his hand. "How did you find the right sponsor?"

"I kept to myself a lot of the time, but Shephard helped." Lucas kissed her forehead. "And so did you."

Rowan glanced my way but not before sitting on a patio love seat. He patted the spot beside him.

Without even thinking twice on it, I joined him. When our knees bumped each other, a sense of peace washed over me at being close to him once again.

"Where do you go for your meetings?" Lily asked, pulling me from my thoughts.

"In the basement of a local church. I guess I need to ask around and do some research on good sponsors? I didn't even know that was a thing." I rubbed the back of my neck, taking a sip of the ice-cold lemonade. It eased my parched throat, but it did nothing for my cravings.

"Yeah, it can be. Sometimes some people take years to find that perfect sponsor. It's hard to trust people," Lucas told me. "I know firsthand how hard it is. You feel alone. You feel like everyone's given up on you because you have relapse after relapse. It's like everyone expects it now and no matter what milestone you reach, if you tell people, they'll only say that you hit it before. You just want people to not give up on you."

A lump burned my throat. I swallowed hard, trying to ignore this sudden rush of feelings but he was right. Fucking hell, he was absolutely right.

"I don't want to relapse," I muttered.

"I don't think anyone does," Lily said gently. "Not anyone who actually wants to overcome their addiction. But you have to remember something, Aiden. You will be battling this for the rest of your life. People like us can't have just social drinks or a joint here and there. Some people mask their addiction with another one and that defeats the purpose. We can't be your sponsors because it's a conflict of interest since you know our son, but we will do what we can to help you in any way."

"Thank you." I blew out a slow breath. "You have helped me more in the last few minutes than my actual sponsor has in the months I was with her."

"Don't settle, Aiden. Search around. Feel people out." Lily gave me a small smile, the lines at the corners of her eyes becoming more pronounced. "You deserve the support. Even if you feel like you're not getting it from your friends and family right now. Just know that they will come around."

"I finally made amends with my parents. Because of Rowan." I held out my hand, needing his touch. When he slipped his fingers between mine, I inched closer to him. "Your son has helped me and I…" I looked up at him then. "Thank you."

"You don't have to thank me, Aiden." He lifted our joined hands. "So, yeah. We're kinda dating now."

"He must really think we're oblivious," Lily told her husband.

"I knew right away." Lucas patted his own back. "Point one for me."

"How did you know?" Rowan asked, looking between his parents.

"Because we saw the way you looked at him." Lily reached for her husband's hand. "Duh."

I listened to their banter; thankful the conversation had become lighter.

Rowan was just like his father with his sense of humor. His mom gave as good as she got, not backing down when Lucas gave her a look. It would only make her laugh harder.

Something crossed my mind then.

Maybe, just maybe, these could be my in-laws one day.

One could only hope.

TWENTY-TWO

ROWAN

AIDEN AND I FELL into an easy routine. It was comfortable and what both of us needed. Every Sunday we would spend time with my family. My parents and my sister welcomed Aiden with open arms. Literally. He couldn't step one foot into my parents' house without being greeted with a hug from either my mom or my sister.

While his parents did the same with me when I finally met them, I was man enough to admit that I had been nervous as well. I had never before met the parents of the person I was sleeping with. Especially when my relationship with Aiden started out backwards. But over the weeks that had past, I became more comfortable with Asher and Meeka Donovan. Not once did they question us being together either. Although his dad and brother did give me the talk.

"*What do you want with Aiden?*" *Ashton asked me. We had met once before when Aiden moved into my apartment. Now we were having dinner at his parents' place, and I finally met his wife as well.*

"*I want a relationship with him.*" *It was the truth. It didn't matter that we started sleeping together right away. Aiden had told me a few times that Ashton had been a player himself, so I knew about his previous escapades before he finally settled down with Tabatha.*

"*Really?*" *Asher, who although was the dad, he could almost pass for their older brother with how much they all looked alike. "Is that all?"*

Under different circumstances, I probably would have laughed at the two men who cornered me when they were finally able to get me away from Aiden, but I didn't. I knew better.

"*Listen.*" *I paused, waiting for them to butt in and say something, but when they didn't, I only continued. "I like Aiden. A lot. Could I see myself falling in love with him? Yes. I could." They didn't need to know I was already in love with him. Aiden needed to find that out first. "I just want to be with him and take this one day at a time. That's it."*

Asher and Ashton looked between each other.

"*Good.*" *Ashton clapped my shoulder, giving it a firm squeeze. "But if you hurt my brother, it's not my dad you'll have to worry about."*

Aiden's brother and father never had to worry about me hurting him. If anyone was going to break someone's heart, it would be him breaking mine.

Miguel had still been quiet and it was annoying. He was plotting and I didn't know what he wanted. Every time I asked him, he just said that he wanted me. It didn't tell me much and I wished he would just come out and say exactly what was on his mind.

After meeting him online and getting paid to send those videos to him, we finally met in person. After a few nights together, I realized that things could have been serious between us but something had told me to get away from him. I had to change my ways. He was toxic, dangerous, and definitely something I didn't need. Since Miguel had kept to himself over the past couple of months, I focused on my relationship with Aiden.

I tried ignoring any questions Aiden had surrounding Miguel. He was worried and I couldn't say I blamed him much.

I never wanted to talk about Miguel, and I always changed the subject as quickly as I could. Even though Aiden had been cool about me selling my body for sex when it came to Miguel, it still bothered me that I did it in the first place. It probably bothered me more than it did Aiden.

Our routine was easy and safe and that was all I wanted. He would go to work. I would go to work. We would both come home around the same time, have dinner together, watch movies, and that was it. We would cuddle. Sometimes more. But what we both needed most was just each other.

We didn't need to have sex. As great as it was. We just needed the companionship, the support and friendship. I needed to feel safe, and I knew he needed the same. I still hadn't met his friends, if you could even call them that. I wasn't sure why. I never asked and I knew that Aiden would include me whenever he felt ready to. It wasn't like he had gone over to their place many times anyway.

One night, I was working late trying to clean up the messes I had caused. I asked Aiden to come over to my store once he was done at his meeting. He had been going to meetings more often and I was proud of him for doing so. He still didn't have a sponsor. Tana had left him alone, but I wasn't sure if he was just telling me that or if she actually did stay away.

It was now pushing eight at night and I was getting antsy.

Something was in the air. Miguel was up to something. I just didn't know what exactly. I tried asking around. I even asked my parents who were retired but liked to play sometimes. My dad especially. I knew he missed the lifestyle of being a hacker, but he had said that once he met my mom, he no longer needed that excitement. But he still did the odd job here and there for friends. Both he and my mom did.

I was twitchy, so to keep my hands busy, I decided to text Aiden.

Me: I'm on edge.

Aiden: I'm on my way.

I sighed, scrubbing a hand down my face. Thank fuck for small mercies.

Heading out of the secret lair as my sister liked to call it, I locked it up and made my way upstairs to my store. I closed up earlier that evening like I always did. It was so I could focus on taking care of the not so legal side of my life. As much as I tried being a better person and earning my money the right way, helping people find shit was what I was good at.

A cab took that moment to pull into the parking lot and I knew this moment with Aiden was going to hurt. I craved his tears, and I needed him to beg me to stop.

Once he slipped out of the vehicle, I stepped outside and leaned against the wall.

His head snapped my way, his eyes never leaving mine as he threw money at the taxi driver.

He mumbled a thank you and as the cab drove away, Aiden stood there. Unsure and stalk still.

"Come here," I demanded, my voice rough.

Like a good little submissive, he did as he was told and stopped a foot away from me. But it wasn't close enough. "Closer."

"What's wrong?" he asked, complying willingly.

"Miguel being quiet is driving me fucking crazy because if he randomly makes an appearance and something happens to you as a result of it, I'll destroy this fucking universe," I said all in one breath.

"Is that all?" Aiden asked, his deep blue eyes twinkling in the dim lighting of the streetlamp that sat only a few feet away in the parking lot.

"I also know you said that you don't give a shit about how I met him, but I need you to reassure me." My body vibrated, my mind racing with thoughts of him leaving me.

"I don't give a shit what you did before me, Rowan."

I grabbed onto the waist of his jeans, pulling him hard against me. "Say it again."

Aiden grunted, reaching his hands beneath my shirt and splaying his fingers over my stomach. "I don't give a shit what you did and I don't judge you. At all. Because I know that all of you is mine."

"Yes." I undid his jeans and pulled down his zipper. "All of me is definitely yours."

"Then prove it." Aiden reached around me and slipped his hands into the waist of my sweatpants. Cupping my ass, he tugged me forward. "Use me to calm yourself down."

Pulling out his thick length, I ran my thumb over the tip of him.

"Use me, Rowan." Aiden's voice dropped an octave. It always did that whenever I had him in my hands.

"Fuck, Aiden." I grabbed onto him, tugging him closer. The movement forced a whimper from his lips. Add to the fact that we were in public, he was hot and throbbing in my hand. Spinning us around, I slammed him up against the wall. "I'm in love with you," I whispered, pushing my waist into the seat of his ass.

His breath caught.

"I don't expect you to say it back, but I needed you to know because I'm about to fuck you like I hate you."

"Geezus, Rowan."

"You know I respect you, right?" I brushed my fingers over the short hair at his nape.

"Yes."

"Good." Ripping his jeans down and over his hips, I landed a palm against his ass cheek. "Stroke your cock, Aiden. Make yourself come but I promise you that I'm not stopping until I fill your ass with my cream."

His breath caught, but he did as he was told. He reached between his legs and started stroking himself. It was a sight I could never get used to. His cock fit perfectly in his hand. It was thick, veiny, and just long enough that I could feel it for days after he fucked me. It had been a while since he dominated me. Maybe I could work him up to the point he had to take over but for now, it was my turn to truly control him. "This is going to hurt."

Pulling my cock out of my pants, I thrust into him before he could prepare himself.

Aiden shouted out, arching away from me.

"That's it, baby boy. Fight me."

Digging his fingers into the brick wall, he shoved back against me but my hold was too strong for him. My fingers dug into his hips, bruising the hard muscles as I fucked my cock into a part of him he had only ever given to me.

"Fight me, Aiden." I slapped his ass again, needing him to try and get away.

"Fuck." With a rough shove, he forced me back. The moment made me fall from his body.

I chuckled, catching him before he could get away from me.

Pulling him away from the wall, I drove back into his body.

He cried out, slapping his hands against the wall.

"That's it. Such a good boy."

Aiden moaned.

Closing the final space between us, I pressed him up against the wall. "Mine."

"Yours," he whispered.

I grinned. "Good boy."

(Aiden)

An hour later and I was curled up on the couch in the basement of Rowan's store. We were in a room I didn't even know existed. It looked like something you would see in a John Wick movie. Especially with all the security Rowan had gone through to get us into this room.

He was currently working away on his computer when he told me he needed to finish something up.

As I watched him, I couldn't help but think back to what he had told me. "Can I ask you something?"

Rowan looked up from his laptop. "You just let me fuck you in public where anyone could have seen us. I think you're entitled to ask me whatever you want."

I laughed, my neck heating. "I was just wondering what made you decide to send Miguel those videos in the first place and get paid for it." I never thought to ask until now. Maybe it should have been something we talked about right when he told me, but now that I realized how much it bugged him, I figured now was the best time to ask.

Rowan closed his laptop and ran a hand through his hair. "It started out with him finding me. I was playing in the dark web, hacking into places I shouldn't have just for shits and giggles because I was bored."

"Really? You did all of that just because you were bored?" As odd as it sounded, it also made sense. Everyone had a vice. Mine just happened to be something that could eventually kill me.

"Yeah." Rowan stood and joined me on the couch. "I meant what I told you. I am in love with you. What Miguel and I had…" A dark shadow passed over his face. "I told him that I wasn't interested in a relationship. I told him this right away. He would contact me whenever he needed a little something and I would in turn do the same. I've done many things but I did not lead him on. He knew right away what he was getting himself into. It still didn't mean that I never developed feelings for him though and I think because of that, maybe he thought I had changed my mind about wanting a relationship with him.

"But when I saw you at that bar, I knew I needed to meet you. Whether you believe in fate or a higher power or not, you have to know that something brought us together. We didn't exchange phone numbers, so when you answered my ad, it was meant to be." He lifted his hand before I could say anything. "I know you've been through a lot, so I don't expect you to say that you love me back. I just needed you to know. I also need you to know that I'm not going anywhere." He took my hands in his, running his thumb along the callouses on my palms from years of hard labor. "Even if you try and fight me, I'll always be here."

"I have feelings for you. You have to know that I do." But could I say that I loved him back? Was that even true? I turned my body toward him, looking down at my hands in his. "I've never been in love, so I don't know what it's supposed to feel like. I do like you though, Rowan. A lot."

Rowan leaned his forehead against mine, letting out a soft sigh. "I know you do."

"Can you be patient with me?"

He cupped my jaw, tilting my head back to meet his stare. "I will always be patient with you. You've given me so much in the short time we've been together. Things I could never repay you for. Things I never knew that I needed in the first place. I can't thank you enough, Aiden."

"I haven't done anything," I murmured.

"Yeah." He gave me a small smirk. "You have." He gave me a soft kiss on the lips. A kiss that was so damn gentle, it forced a lump in my throat. Especially when most times he was usually aggressive and took what he wanted.

"So…" I looked around us. "What exactly is this room used for?"

Rowan chuckled. "Uh…it's a safe place. The only other person who's been in here is my sister. My parents know about it, but they act like it doesn't exist, so they stay away. The work I do, besides selling items in my store, is not legal, Aiden. I'm trying to clean that up but it's taking a while. And it may never stop. Can you handle that?"

"You mean, can I handle the fact that my boyfriend does illegal shit to get by?"

Something flashed in his eyes like it always does whenever I referred to him as my *boyfriend*.

"Yeah." His gaze dropped to my mouth.

"Whatever you do to get by, is none of my business, Rowan." I leaned back against the couch, stretching out my legs in front of me. Every inch of me hurt from the rough way he had used me when I first showed up tonight, but it was a pain that felt good at the same time. And one I never wanted to be rid of.

"It should be your business though." He trailed a finger down my forearm, a path of goose bumps following behind it. "If this gets any more serious and I think it will." His eyes popped to mine. "I don't want to keep anything from you."

I turned toward him, lifting my knee onto the couch and taking his hands in mine. "Rowan, I—"

Suddenly, a bang sounded. It wasn't loud since Rowan explained that this room was specially made to drown out noise, but I still heard it off in the distance.

"What is it?" he asked, frowning.

"You didn't hear that?" I released his hands and stood. "I heard a bang or something that sounded like it. I don't know. This room is too damn quiet."

"A bang," he repeated, walking behind his desk. He wiggled the mouse and clicked a few keys. "I don't see anything."

"I'm telling you I heard something." It may not have been loud, not from this room anyway, but it still set me on edge.

"I believe you, but I just don't know what it could be. But…"

When his voice trailed off, I looked at him over my shoulder. "What?"

"Like I told you, my store is only a front for the real shit I do. I've been trying to get out, but some people aren't happy about that. Maybe they're letting me know just how unhappy they truly are."

A thought came to me, forcing a lead weight in the pit of my stomach. "What if it's Miguel?"

Rowan's head snapped up, his mouth falling open, almost like he was about to argue. But when he only snapped it shut, he muttered a curse. "I'd say that you're wrong, but I don't know anymore. Anything is possible." He closed his laptop and stomped toward the wall I was standing in front of. "You never saw this."

"I was in the Navy, Rowan. I didn't say shit when I was taken. I think I know how to keep a secret."

Before I knew what was happening, Rowan thrust his arm out and caught me by the shirt. He pulled me against him, his dark eyes suddenly furious. "You do not joke about that shit. Ever. You hear me?"

"Rowan, I wasn't joking but I was trying to make light—"

"Never." He released me roughly. "Or I'll kick your ass and you won't like it."

I scoffed, crossing my arms under my chest. "I'd like to see you try."

"I'll deal with you later," he grumbled. "I need to figure out what the hell is going on and exactly what you heard."

What happened next, was like it came right out of a movie. Rowan pressed a button on a square box that sat on the tiled wall. A panel opened beside it, revealing quite the collection of weapons.

I whistled, moving in front of the wall of heavy machinery. "Expecting a war, baby?"

Rowan came up to my side, placing a peck on my cheek. "Can never be too careful anymore."

TWENTY-THREE

ROWAN

MY WORDS WERE TRUE. Sure, I probably had too much protection, but when it came to those I loved and with the people I had done work for over the years, one could never be too safe.

When Aiden told me he heard a noise, it took everything in me not to spring into action and call for backup. Even if it was only Miguel, the man was unstable. That had been one reason I didn't want to be with him. Aiden may have had his own personal shit to deal with and I would be there every step of the way to help him through it, but Miguel? He was unhinged. And not in a dark sexy way either.

While Aiden checked out what I had in stock, I went back to my computer to take a glance at the security cameras once again.

My stomach twisted, the hairs on my body tingling as I watched the man I had left months ago, stare up at the camera. I had never brought him to this room. Never even told him about it. But Miguel knew that besides soliciting myself for sex, I helped people find out information. I did more than the police ever could since they had a lot of red tape they had to go through. There was only one group of people I would continue to help outside of friends and family. I had been tempted to make a phone call, but Miguel was moving things faster than I would have liked.

"Rowan?"

I looked up, finding Aiden standing there with a shotgun in hand, the barrel resting against his shoulder.

"It's Miguel…" he paused. "Isn't it?"

I didn't want this. I didn't want any of this. I tried to be a good guy and told Miguel right away that I just wanted sex. He still wanted to pay for it because it had been a kink of his.

"The last time I saw Miguel, I threw a wad of one-hundred-dollar bills in his face after I fucked him in a room full of people." I stood up straight. "I find out information for people. People who can't go to the police for fear of getting thrown in jail. If I got caught, I'd end up in jail for life." I stepped around the desk and went up to Aiden. "I helped a woman find her ex-husband so she could get back at him for years of abuse. The divorce wasn't enough for her. She had to kill him."

Aiden's eyes darkened watching me become unraveled, but he needed to know. He needed to know my truths and everything that went on in my fucked-up brain.

"She told me too. She told me every sordid detail, Aiden. And you know what? I didn't go to the police. I didn't tell on her. I kept her secret safe. This whole time."

"Why are you telling me this?" Aiden asked, his eyes moving back and forth over my face as I got closer.

"Because I need you to know that the man you have feelings for, the man who is in love with you, is not a good guy. I try to be. Fuck me, do I ever try to be but—"

"Stop." Aiden closed that final space between us and captured my shirt in his fist. He crushed his mouth to mine. "You *are* a good guy. You've just done bad things. So have I. Now shut the fuck up and let's see what the hell is going on so we can go home."

I stared at him, wishing I could fall to his feet and beg for him to fuck every single inch of me. But before I could even hint at such a thing, a bang sounded and this time I heard it.

"I knew I wasn't losing my damn mind," Aiden grumbled, rushing to the door.

Another bang erupted through the building, shaking the walls around us. We were in the basement and while usually it would have been safe for us, we had nowhere to go. We were stuck and I didn't know how to get us out if we were barricaded in.

Grabbing a 9mm, I shoved it into the seat of my pants at the small of my back. Heading toward Aiden, I was about to push him away to unlock the door when an explosion sounded.

Thankfully the door was reinforced, so nothing happened. The noise was just loud, and it made me nervous as fuck.

"We have to get out of here." Aiden spun on me. "Unlock the door."

I did as I was told and entered in the security code to get us out of this room. We quickly rushed out of it and headed up to the main floor of the shop. But nothing could have prepared me for what I saw next.

Everything was gone. Literally.

The items I had spent years collecting, were strewn about on the floor, most were shattered and broken. Even though it wasn't my main source of income, it hurt. Seeing my life laid out like this, fuck me, did it ever hurt.

"Rowan." Aiden grabbed my hand, leading me out of the shop. The smoke was heavy, forcing us both into coughing fits, but once we reached outside the fresh air helped clear our lungs.

"This is…" My throat tightened.

"I'm so sorry." Aiden kept hold of my hand, pulling me away from the wreckage. "I'll call 911."

"You'll do no such thing."

Aiden's head whipped around at the sound of the deep voice, but I didn't need to look to know who it was.

"Miguel," Aiden whispered. Even though he had never seen what he looked like, it didn't matter. Miguel hadn't been a problem. Not until now and I didn't know why.

"It seems we finally meet," Miguel said, his voice smooth and silky. It held a slight accent, probably from somewhere in Europe but I didn't know because he never told me. He wanted me but he never told me anything about his life. There were too many damn secrets between us. But I had been blinded by the fact that he had been interested in me in the first place. Now that I was with Aiden, I was thankful that I ended things with Miguel when I did.

When I finally turned around, my chest tightened at the sight of him. His dark hair was a mess of curls, his eyes were sunken in with graying circles under them. The clothes he wore hung off of him. He had been skinny to begin with but now, he just looked sick.

"What's happened to you?" I asked him, truly caring. I didn't want to hurt him and I never wished any ill will on him either. I just wanted him to leave us alone and move on with his life.

Miguel shifted from foot to foot, swaying a little at the movement. His head twitched side to side, soft murmuring sounds leaving him.

"He's on something," Aiden said, low enough for only me to hear.

"Let me help you," I told Miguel, taking a step in his direction. "I can take you somewhere."

Miguel's eyes snapped to mine. They were glassy and unfocused.

"Help me," he repeated. "You want to help me." He laughed, the sound high-pitched. He was strung the fuck out and it made me nervous as hell.

I stepped in front of Aiden, shielding him. He could handle himself, but this was on me. I brought Miguel into his life, so I would protect him at all costs. No matter what.

"Did you blow up my store?" I asked Miguel even though I already knew the answer.

He began muttering incoherent sounds and words I couldn't make out. The longer he stood there, the more my skin began to crawl.

"We need to call the police," Aiden said from behind me.

That seemed to snap Miguel to attention. "Police? You think calling the police will protect you?"

"Protect us from what, Miguel? What's going on?" Maybe if I continued asking him questions, it would delay the inevitable. He was here for a reason, but I just didn't know what that reason was.

(Aiden)

This guy was dangerous.

From the brief time I had gone to AA meetings, I saw drug addicts like him hanging around. They never went inside but they were there. It was as if they were waiting for a higher power to pull them into the building. Or they were waiting for someone to tell them that they didn't need these meetings and that they didn't actually have a problem.

While I was only addicted to alcohol, I knew that I could become like Miguel. It didn't matter the substance. Having an addictive personality, even if it came on later in life, made it so you couldn't have a social drink or that one puff to take the edge off. You fought for more. You lost family, friends, everything you worked for in life. You lost it once that substance took over.

As I watched Rowan and Miguel have a silent standoff, I searched within myself for a hint of jealousy. When it never came and something else took hold instead, I knew. I was in love with Rowan. It all made sense now.

But before I could even hint at such a thing, especially given the circumstances, Miguel pulled something from the back of his jeans.

"I love you, Rowan," he said, his voice cracking. "I've loved you this whole time, but you never noticed. You didn't care."

"I told you that I didn't want a relationship," Rowan said gently.

"Then why the fuck are you with him and not me?" he roared, his face going red. "What makes him so damn special?"

"Miguel, listen, I'm sorry." Rowan held his hands out in surrender. "I really am. I never meant to lead you on. I thought telling you that I didn't want anything more than just sex, would be enough. I thought you would understand. You said you were fine with us just having some fun. No strings. Those were your words."

Miguel's eyes welled. He lifted his arm, holding a pistol.

My stomach sunk.

Rowan muttered a curse. "Don't do this. We can talk this out."

"Talk this out." Miguel laughed, shaking his head. "We can't talk this out. Not while you're with him."

I took a step around Rowan when Miguel aimed the gun at me. Thrusting up my hands, I tried thinking of what I could say that would calm him down. But he was already so far gone, no one would be able to talk him out of doing whatever it was he had set out to do.

"You don't want to do this," I told him.

"You don't know what the fuck I want to do or not want to do. This is all your fault anyway." Beads of sweat formed on Miguel's forehead. He pulled at his collar, whatever he was on, clearly making him uncomfortable and hinting for him to get more.

"Tell me it was you who blew up my store." As soon as those words left Rowan's lips, sirens sounded. "Tell me," he demanded.

Miguel looked around frantically. He didn't have a lot of time. When his eyes locked with mine, everything inside of me screamed that we wouldn't make it out of this unharmed. If even alive at all. My thoughts quickly traveled to my parents and how I was finally getting along with them once again. How I had started going back to AA meetings and was on a search for a decent sponsor. How life was finally starting to work out even though my head was still a damn mess.

"I did this…" He paused. "I did this because of you." Miguel cocked the pistol and a shot sounded.

The next thing I knew, I was shoved. Hard.

The shot had been so loud that I was momentarily brought back to a time where I never thought I would survive. I had been through a lot, like Rowan pointed out. Even though I didn't know him at the time, I survived because of him.

"Fuck," Miguel's whimpered cry pulled me from my thoughts.

Agony erupted from the back of my head, the ringing in my ears getting louder and louder.

I blinked a couple of times, trying to get rid of that damn noise in my head. Every inch of me hurt, something heavy laying on top of me. It was a body. A body I knew. My heart started racing. No. No it couldn't be.

"I didn't mean to," Miguel's shaky voice erupted through me.

Shaking my head, I took a deep breath, the ringing finally dissipating.

Pushing the heavy weight off of me, a whimpered cry left me when I saw Rowan with his eyes closed. Blood seeped out of a gaping hole in the side of his neck.

"What the fuck did you do?" I yelled, covering the wound with my hands. The blood wouldn't stop. It kept spilling between my fingers. I had to stop the bleeding.

Ripping off my hoodie, I pressed the fabric against the side of his throat.

"I didn't…I was aiming for you," came Miguel's broken response.

I ignored him and tried to stop the bleeding in my boyfriend's neck. "Call 911," I shouted.

Miguel didn't listen and kept muttering how he didn't mean to. How he wasn't aiming for Rowan but for me instead.

Ignoring him, I pulled my cell from my pocket and dialed 911. I was in a fog as the dispatcher asked questions. I must have given the appropriate answers when she told me the paramedics were on their way along with the police and firefighters. She had insisted that I don't hang up, but I did anyway because I needed to focus on Rowan. The man I had fallen in love with. The man I didn't know I needed.

No matter how much I tried pushing him away, he never gave up. He made me see that we were perfect together. That this was meant to be.

As the sirens neared, they became louder. Miguel continued mumbling things I couldn't hear. All I could focus on was Rowan and how he was bleeding so damn much, every thought I had was of him not making it.

"You can't die on me, Rowan. You can't. I love you." I kissed his forehead. "You hear me? I love you."

"You love him?" Miguel's words were shaky. "You love him," he repeated.

Holding my hands to Rowan's wound, I looked over at Miguel. "Yes, I do. And he loves me." I knew then that I shouldn't have said anything. That he was mentally unstable and there was no guessing as to what he would do or how he would react. But I couldn't take back my words. They were said. They were the truth. But the reaction they caused in Miguel was something I would never forget. No matter how hard I tried.

A pained cry left him, his cheeks going red. Much to my surprise, he lifted his hand and put the barrel of the gun in his mouth.

I looked away as the gunshot rang out. It made me jump even though I knew what was coming. I could hear his body hit the ground in a crumpled heap. He would no longer be a problem and it made my chest ache. I didn't want this. When Rowan woke up, I would have to tell him, and I wasn't sure how he would take it.

An ambulance pulled into the driveway, followed by police cars. Voices sounded out, some shouting, some gentle. They were talking to me, trying to get me to tell them what had happened. Fire trucks arrived, the firefighters taking care of Rowan's store and what was left of it. I looked around me, watching the emergency services do their job but I couldn't respond. Words were lost on my tongue. Tonight, wasn't supposed to happen. Not like this.

A heavy hand landed on my shoulder, pulling me away from Rowan and I didn't even struggle. I watched the EMTs work on my boyfriend. I didn't know if he would make it. Could life be that cruel to take something away from me I never knew I needed in the first place? Could a higher power be that evil to give me something, the greatest thing I had ever received, and take it away like it was some sick joke?

"Please," I heard myself say but no one responded. How could they? It wasn't like they knew what I was talking about.

When I saw Rowan being placed on a stretcher, I rushed toward him. But I didn't make it very far when two cops stepped in front of me, stopping me from getting to the man I wanted to spend the rest of my life with.

"We have some questions," one officer said.

They had questions, so that meant they needed some answers. Answers I wouldn't be able to provide.

They threw question after question at me.

What happened?

How did I know Rowan?

Did I shoot him?

What reason did Miguel have for shooting himself?

My stomach twisted at that. I would have to tell Rowan. Even though they were no longer together and hadn't been for some time, I knew that it would still hurt nonetheless. Rowan didn't wish any harm on the guy. Neither did I. I didn't know him. I never wanted to know him. But I didn't wish him dead either.

The officers insisted on bringing me to the station. When someone was shot and another committed suicide, it didn't look good for the person who survived. I was brought back to the last mission I had gone on before most of my squad had been killed. I survived that too. But I never asked for it. I never asked to be alone in this whole thing.

When I was brought to the station, even though I tried protesting, the officers threw question after question at me. Some I answered, most I didn't because I didn't know how to answer them. I didn't know why Miguel did what he did. He said he was aiming for me. What good that would do was beyond me.

Especially when it wouldn't have convinced Rowan to be with Miguel in the first place.

What felt like hours later, I was finally released on condition that I wouldn't leave the state anytime soon.

The only place I was heading to was the hospital. I wasn't sure if Rowan's parents were called. I hoped they were because I didn't have a way of contacting them myself.

When I arrived at the hospital, I checked in with the front desk. After I was given the information on what floor Rowan was on, I headed up to it, but I felt like a zombie. I didn't even remember getting there. People looked at me funny and I had no idea why until I passed a window and saw my reflection. Looking down at myself, I noticed the blood on my shirt and hands. I wiped them on my jeans, but it only seemed to make it worse.

My breath caught in my throat. My knees wobbled beneath me. They threatened to give out, taking my body down with them. It would probably feel good. That pain of hitting the floor. It would numb how I was feeling but, in all reality, I wasn't sure how I was feeling. I was scared. Of course, I was scared. If Rowan was taken from me before we could even begin our relationship the way we had set out to do, I wasn't sure what it would do to me.

"Aiden?"

My head snapped up, finding Rowan's parents and sister, standing by a desk.

"I'm sorry," was all I said.

Rowan's mom rushed toward me. She threw herself around my middle, hugging me with everything in her. "Don't be sorry. Please don't be sorry."

"But I am. If I wasn't there…if Rowan and I…Miguel wouldn't have…" I couldn't get the words out, my sentences broken and jumbled. "He can't leave me."

"Aiden, you did nothing wrong."

I shook my head at Lucas's words. Even though they were kind and gentle, it still didn't mean that I didn't feel like this was my fault. If I never would have called about that ad or fallen in love with Rowan in the first place, he wouldn't be fighting for his life right now. It was my fault.

All of it.

Was.

My.

Fault.

"Please, Aiden." Lily released me as Lucas came up behind her. She turned to her husband. "Tell him."

"It's not your fault." Lucas ran a hand over his shaved head. "We met Miguel once. It was only in passing. Rowan didn't want us to get to know him because it wasn't serious. He also spoke to us a few times about how his mental health was unstable."

"I should have noticed the signs. I should have insisted that Rowan do something more than just telling Miguel to leave him…us…alone. I should have…" I was on the verge of losing it. I knew that. But until Rowan was fine and back in my arms, I would be questioning every single decision I made in the last twenty-four hours.

"Excuse us."

We turned at the sound of a woman in a suit coming toward us, followed by a police officer who had a scowl on his face.

"I'm Detective Jessica Baldwin," the woman said, introducing herself. "And this is Officer Andy Jaxon."

Rowan's parents introduced themselves while I stood back. I could only imagine that the detective and officer were there for me.

"You must be Aiden." Detective Baldwin glanced my way.

I nodded, shoving my hands in my pockets.

"Would you mind if we ask you some questions?" Although her question came across kind, there was a hardness to her just the same.

"I already spent hours at the station," I told her. "What more could you possibly need to know?"

She gave me a small smile. "We—"

"We want to make sure that what you told the officers at the station is the same thing you tell us." Officer Jaxon jutted his chin. "Gotta make sure you aint lyin', kid."

Detective Baldwin glared at him, clearly unhappy that she was interrupted. "I got this, Andy." She muttered a curse and took a step toward me. "Listen, I know this is a difficult time for all of you. We're wanting to rule everything out."

"Miguel bombed the store and was outside when we evacuated. He aimed his gun at me, Rowan pushed me away, and got shot instead. Then Miguel killed himself as a result of it. Nothing more. Nothing less." I wasn't sure what the hell these cops were wanting to know.

"Are you sure it was just that?" Detective Baldwin started walking away. "Let's go somewhere private," she said, instead of waiting for me to answer.

Looking back at Rowan's parents, I wished they would tell me it was okay. That everything would be fine. I should call my parents. My brother. Someone. I didn't want to deal with this alone.

Lily frowned, chewing her bottom lip.

Lucas scowled but nodded.

I drew in a sharp breath, turned on my heel, and headed the same way Detective Baldwin went.

As I neared, I overheard voices coming from the waiting room.

"You don't need to be here, Andy." That was obviously Detective Baldwin speaking.

"Where you go, I go," Officer Jaxon told her.

"Right." She scoffed. "I'm going to go get Aiden."

I took that as my chance and entered the room as Andy grabbed Jessica's arm and pulled her against him. She gasped, slapping her hands against his chest.

He smirked.

I knew that look. Rowan had given it me so many times, I had it locked safely in my memories.

"Stop." Jessica pushed away from him before he could do whatever it was he had intended to do.

Clearing my throat, I entered the room.

Jessica's head whipped around, her cheeks going pink, while Andy only looked at her.

"Nice of you to join us." She coughed. "Please sit."

TWENTY-FOUR

AIDEN

ROWAN WAS STILL IN critical condition. But the police ruled me out as a suspect. They determined that it was an ex who was jealous. Which was what I had told them in the first place.

When they left, I called my parents.

"Hey, Son," Dad answered. "How are–"

"Rowan was shot," I blurted.

"Where are you?" he asked, his voice rough.

"I'm at the hospital," my voice wavered. "His parents and sister are here. I just…I need…"

"I'm on my way."

When Dad hung up, I dropped the phone onto the chair beside me and slumped in the seat. Lucas, Lily, and Ettie were with Rowan. Even though he was still in ICU, Lucas made some threats and eventually, they were allowed to see their son and brother.

"Aiden."

My eyes popped open, not realizing I had closed them. I didn't know how much time had passed but when I saw my dad standing at the entrance to the waiting room, my chest tightened. My eyes welled, a hard lump burning my throat.

"Come here," he said gently. Although things had been better between us, we still tiptoed around each other. But none of that mattered. Right now, I just needed my dad.

Jumping from the chair, I rushed to him and threw myself around my father.

He returned the embrace, squeezing me hard. "I'm here."

That was when I broke.

Bone crushing sobs tore through me. Images of losing Rowan kept flashing in my mind. I wouldn't know how to live life without him. He came into my world like a violent storm, taking all of my destruction with him. He made everything better. He made *me* better. A better man. A better person.

When I calmed down, I pulled away from Dad and wiped my face. That was when I noticed the dried blood on my hands. Rowan's blood. His life force.

Dad grabbed my shaking hands and led me out of the waiting room. He walked me to the nearby bathroom and gently ushered me inside. Through all of my actions, I couldn't focus and kept thinking that Rowan wasn't going to make it.

Dad turned on the water in the sink and began washing my hands. It wouldn't help when I knew that the blood had been there in the first place. It was all I could see in my mind's eye. But it was a start. Wasn't it?

What if Rowan didn't make it? Could I survive that loss? I was already an alcoholic because of shit I had been through in the Navy. Losing Rowan would set me back. Maybe even worse. I knew that. I wasn't stupid.

"Aiden."

I met Dad's gaze in the mirror. Lines sat at the corners of his eyes. Salt and pepper sprinkled throughout his hair and beard. I noticed then that it looked like he had lost some weight.

"Are you okay?" I heard myself ask.

Dad's eyes widened a bit before he shook it off. "Why do you ask?"

"Maybe it's because we haven't spent much time together. Not until recently. But you look like you've lost weight." I shrugged. "Maybe I'm wrong."

Dad smiled, turned off the water, and handed me some paper towels. "I'm fine."

"Would you tell me if you weren't?"

He opened his mouth to say something, probably to argue, but let out a sigh instead. "Yeah, I would. I am fine though, Aiden. I got really sick there for a few weeks. Just a nasty cold that turned into the flu, which then turned to strep. So, I lost a few pounds because I could barely swallow anything with how my throat felt. But it was nothing serious. It just kicked my ass."

Relief flooded through me. As much as my dad and I didn't get along, even though we were finally working on it, I didn't want anything to happen to him either.

"Good, I'm glad." And I was.

We left the bathroom and walked in silence back to the waiting room.

"Rowan saved my life," I finally told him. I explained about Miguel and what had happened and how he had blown up Rowan's store and shot him instead of me like he had intended. Then I told him how Miguel shot himself because guilt controlled his actions.

"Fucking hell." Dad shoved a hand through his hair.

"I just…I can't lose him." My voice wavered, my eyes welling once again.

"Aiden."

My head snapped up as Lucas came into the room.

He glanced at Dad, a frown forming on his face. "Ashton. It's been a while."

"It has." Dad stood and went up to Rowan's father, holding out his hand.

They shook, which turned into a one-armed hug.

"Sorry, it's under these circumstances but it's good to see you," Dad said, looking back at me.

"You two know each other?" I had no idea.

"We do." Lucas nodded once. "Although the wife and I like to stick to ourselves these days."

"I get that. We'll have to get together," Dad suggested. "I think the ladies would like that."

"I agree." Lucas glanced my way. "I thought you looked familiar when Rowan brought you to the house. Now I know why."

I wished I could have asked them how they met but I needed to know how Rowan was doing.

"How's Rowan?" I asked, not wanting to interrupt their little reunion but I had to know that the man I wanted to spend my life with was okay. That he would make it through this.

"He's stable but it's still touch and go," Lucas answered, a dark shadow passing over his face.

I looked down at my hands, they were clean thanks to my dad helping me wash them, but I could still see the blood. Rowan's blood. And it was something I would never get out of my head. No matter how much I tried.

Touch and go.

Three words that held so much weight. They took my breath away.

"Can I see him?" I asked Lucas. "I know it's supposed to be family only—"

"You are family," Lucas reminded me. "I should have brought you to him a while ago, but Lily isn't taking it well."

"I understand." I looked down at my hands again, expecting there to be blood.

"Go see him," Dad insisted.

"I'll take you to him and bring my wife to get some coffee, so you can have some privacy with him. But if anything changes, you come get us."

"I will."

"I wish…" Lucas hesitated.

Dad stood and clapped his shoulder. "I get it."

A shuttered breath left Rowan's dad.

My chest tightened. "I wish I could avenge Rowan," I blurted.

Both of the older men looked at me.

"I know I shouldn't speak ill of the dead. Trust me. I know that. But Miguel wasn't well. He was unstable."

"I tried telling Rowan this in the beginning even though Miguel didn't do anything drastic at first. Not like this. I had a feeling, but both Lily and I thought maybe I was being paranoid." Lucas ran a hand over his buzzed head. "I guess I was wrong."

"I wish…I wish I could bring Miguel back to life so I could kill him myself." I waited, expecting Dad and Lucas to tell me I was crazy. To call the cops and tell them that I was losing my mind. To lock me up and throw away the key.

But instead, Lucas closed the distance between us and wrapped me up in his thick arms. "You took the words right out of my head. My wife has helped me be a better person. A better man." He leaned back, looking down at me. "But this is our son. Our only son. This isn't right. And I feel guilty because I want to do something, but I can't because Miguel is gone. It's like he took the easy way out. And I know it's not right to think that, but he almost killed my son. He tried killing you."

Dad muttered a curse.

Even though I knew that was Miguel's intention, hearing someone else say it didn't make it better, but it did help me realize that maybe I wasn't losing my mind.

"Let's take you to Rowan. Maybe if you're there and you talk to him, he'll wake up," Lucas suggested.

Even though he was heavily medicated, I needed to hear him talk. I needed to hear him and his sick, twisted humor. I needed *him*.

Lucas sighed, running a hand over his shaved head again and I noticed he did that whenever he was uncomfortable or didn't know what to say. "I need my son to wake up."

"I know." I took a deep breath. "Me too." I wished I had better words for him. Better words of encouragement. I wished there was something I could do but instead, I let Lucas lead me out of the room. I paused at the doorway, looking back at dad. "Are you staying?"

Dad nodded. "I'll stay as long as you want me to."

"I'd like you to stay. For a little bit anyway."

Dad nodded again and sat. "I'll call your mom and let her know where I am. You take all the time you need."

I joined Lucas and he brought me to Rowan's room. I tried mentally preparing myself, but I still wasn't expecting to see what I saw. Even though I knew that it wouldn't be a pretty sight, seeing Rowan in that bed, made him appear smaller. Even though he technically wasn't.

Tubes were sticking out of his arms.

A tube to help him breathe was down his throat. The sounds of the beeping machines made my heart pick up speed.

Before Lucas could say anything, I rushed to Rowan and dropped to my knees beside his bed. Grabbing his hand, I kissed his bloody knuckles.

I wasn't sure where the blood came from. Maybe it was his own. Maybe he had scraped his knuckles when he pushed me out of the way and fell on top of me. I didn't know. Maybe I would never know. All that mattered was that Rowan was alive. But I still needed him to open his eyes. I needed to tell him that I loved him.

Not caring in the least that Lucas was still in the room, I rose to my full height and leaned over Rowan, placing a soft kiss on his forehead.

A soft sob replaced the quiet of the room.

Lily was sitting in a chair on the other side of the bed with Ettie standing at her side. I wasn't thinking straight and didn't even see either of them when I came into the room.

I was vaguely aware of Lucas ushering his girls out of the room to give us some privacy. It was on the tip of my tongue to tell them to stay. They were Rowan's family after all, but I couldn't bring myself to do it.

"I need you to open your eyes," I told Rowan, tears rolling down my cheeks. "I need you to know that I love you. I need you to know that you are it for me. You're stubborn. You didn't give up on me and I can't thank you enough for that. But I need you to open your eyes, Rowan. Please open your eyes." My words came out jumbled. I was a mess, waiting for him to look at me and talk to me. To tell me that it would be okay.

What the hell was Miguel thinking? He had aimed for me, pulled the trigger, Rowan shoved me out of the way and got hit once. But I remembered hearing two shots.

Why would Miguel shoot again?

You would think that he would have noticed that he hit the wrong person. Unless he had intended to hit Rowan all along. I didn't know. And we would never know. But I still wished I could give Rowan the answers. He might not even care. I wasn't sure. But it was enough to drive me mad.

Pulling up the chair beside his bed, I sat and held his hand in mine. I whispered words to him that I hoped he could hear. I told him how much I loved him. How much he had saved me. Because of him, I didn't have a drink in months. As much as I wanted to, especially at this moment, I didn't have a drop. It was like I was too focused on him and us.

Maybe there wasn't a reason for it. I could almost hear him saying that he wouldn't want me to drink alcohol just because of him. It wasn't just because of him. I would tell him that as well. He was definitely a big part of it though. It helped that he was patient and that he knew what it was like to live with this disease even though he didn't have it himself. He grew up around it.

I wasn't sure how much time had passed. It felt like forever since Rowan was shot and ended up in the hospital, fighting for his life.

People came into the room. Nurses and doctors checked on him, but nothing had changed. I was vaguely aware of his sister hugging me. But I was in a fog, and I couldn't focus on anything but the man laying in the bed next to me.

I longed for him to wake up and tell me that he loved me. It took everything in me not to shake him or even slap him, just to see if I could get some sort of reaction from him.

It was almost like he was in a coma. The doctor said he wasn't. They used a lot of other medical terminology I didn't understand, nor did I want to. I just wanted Rowan better, even if he wasn't one-hundred-percent when he came out of this.

I just needed him to wake up. We could deal with everything else later.

My dad spent as much time with me as he could, but he eventually insisted that I go home and take a shower.

I didn't even remember doing that. All I could remember was sitting beside Rowan and praying that he would make it out of this.

A couple of days after he was shot, I walked into his room and found him staring at me.

My knees almost buckled at the sight of his eyes boring into mine.

"Come here," he said, his voice rough and gravelly.

My eyes welled. My chest tightening as a part of me had thought that I would never hear his voice again.

"I said, come here." That demanding tone of his almost forced me to the floor. But even though he wanted me closer, I couldn't move.

Was I dreaming?

Was this a messed-up nightmare?

Was life playing a trick on me?

Before he could speak again, I rushed to him and threw myself in his arms.

He held me tight as I cried and thanked whoever was listening that they brought him back to me.

"I'm fine," he told me, his voice thick, but he wasn't stupid.

And neither was I.

He chanced fate and survived.

"I'm sorry," I said, not exactly sure what I was apologizing for.

"Why are you sorry?"

Instead of answering, I held him tighter and pushed my face into the crook of his neck. I breathed him in. He smelled like the hospital but there was still a hint of him there. A hint of the spicy scent that made up him.

Rowan held me tight as I kept mumbling how sorry I was.

"Stop," he demanded gently.

But I couldn't. I held him tight, needing more than just a hug. I needed to take him home. I needed his bed. Our bed. I needed him. Not sex. I just needed…more.

"Baby." He pulled back, cupping my face. "I'm fine. I promise I'm fine. But you have nothing to be sorry about."

"Miguel shot himself. He was aiming for me. You saved me. If it wasn't for me, he'd be alive. I just…I'm sorry." My words came out in a rush.

Rowan sighed, moving over in the bed. He winced at the movement but patted the spot beside him anyway.

There wasn't a lot of room, so I didn't budge.

"Get in the bed with me, Aiden, before I make you."

His rough tone sent a shiver down my spine, but I did as he said. I didn't want him to hurt himself any more.

Rowan wrapped his arm around my shoulders, placing a soft peck on my temple. "You have nothing to be sorry about and before you argue, let me tell you something. Miguel has always had issues. I told you that. But he's threatened to take his life before. I never told you that part because I didn't want you to worry. You had enough shit to deal with."

"You shouldn't have made that call yourself, Rowan." I sat up, dropping my head in my hands. The bed was too damn small.

"Aiden, look at me."

I glanced at him over my shoulder.

"I meant what I said." He shifted in the bed. "I love you."

"I love you too," I whispered.

(Rowan)

"Say that again." I wasn't sure if I heard him correctly.

"I love you," Aiden repeated, louder that time.

Every nerve ending in my body, tingled with delight that I had finally made this man, this beautiful broken man, fall in love with me. But as much as I wanted to celebrate on that, we had to talk about this guilt he was feeling first.

"Listen to me." I sat up as best I could, and reached for the back of his neck. Running my thumb along his pulse point, my dick twitched when he shivered. At least that part of me was still working. "I should have told you how sick Miguel was from the very beginning. I'm sorry I didn't. That's on me. And yes, before you say anything, he shouldn't have tried to shoot you."

"You saved me," Aiden said, his breath wavering. "I can't ever repay you for that."

I raised an eyebrow. "You don't have to repay shit, Aiden. You should know that. I would have done it, no matter who it was."

"So, you're telling me that I'm not special?"

"What?" I shook my head. "No. Fuck. That's not what I meant."

Aiden smiled, a light laugh leaving him. "I'm kidding."

"Geezus, fuck, Aiden." I squeezed the back of his neck. "You drive me fucking crazy."

"Good," he whispered.

We sat like that, in silence, and just enjoyed each other's company. It was calming in a way. Aiden eased the constant need for mass destruction rushing through me. My parents always told me I was a hothead.

Tonight, shouldn't have happened. Or the night before. Maybe it was longer. I couldn't remember. Time was lost on me. But I was alive. And Miguel wasn't.

I never wanted that for him. I tried being his friend. Maybe I shouldn't have. Maybe I led him on and wasn't aware of it.

Did I accidentally make promises to him that I couldn't keep, and he somehow lost it?

Maybe he took it to mean that I did actually want to be with him. Maybe he assumed that Aiden and I would share him, since it had been something I talked about before. But that was before I met Aiden. That was before he told me that he was down for anything but sharing. Which was fine with me. I was possessive as fuck anyway, but I also knew at the same time, that even if we did invite a third party into our little duo, it would always end up being just Aiden and me in the end.

"You're thinking," Aiden muttered. "You're thinking very loudly actually."

"Like you, I'm having a bit of survivor's guilt," I confessed.

He sighed, running a hand through his hair. "It sucks, doesn't it?"

"Yeah, it does." I linked my fingers in his, running my thumb over his calloused palm.

The hospital staff came and went. They reassured me that I would be discharged the following day. I couldn't wait because I really needed to get Aiden back in my bed and start living our lives as an actual couple. I wanted to take him on dates, celebrate anniversaries and our birthdays, and more. I wanted to get to know his family better and finally meet his friends and for him to do the same with mine.

Once it was time to be released from the hospital, a knock suddenly sounded on the door. Aiden and I looked at each other. He only shrugged.

A woman entered the room, followed by a police officer.

"Rowan, it's good to see you up and about," the woman said, giving me a small smile.

"Do I know you?" She was vaguely familiar, both of them were, but I couldn't place where I had seen them before.

"I'm Detective Jessica Baldwin and this is Officer Andy Jaxon," she said, introducing both her and the cop. "We came in here as soon as the doctor said you were awake. You probably don't remember much of that."

"No, I don't." I only remembered the past few days. Nothing earlier than that.

"I just wanted to wish you well and give you this." Detective Baldwin handed me a USB stick.

"What's this?" I asked her.

"I don't know but we found it in an envelope in Miguel's apartment and it was addressed to you," she explained.

"You never checked it?" I looked between Aiden and them.

"Listen, kid." Officer Jaxon took a step forward. "You had some heavy-duty security at your store. It caught everything on camera, so it was proven that Miguel did in fact shoot himself and that you saved Aiden here. Anything more than that, is none of our business."

"Why?" I frowned, feeling like something was up. "I mean, you must want to know what's on this. What's the catch?"

"Rowan," Aiden muttered.

A shared look passed between Detective Baldwin and Officer Jaxon before they looked back at me.

"You kids have been through a lot." Detective Baldwin nodded toward the USB drive in my hand. "Take this as a sign of good faith."

"That means, don't leave town." Officer Jaxon turned on his heel and made his way toward the door. "Jess."

Her cheeks reddened but she followed the cop, leaving Aiden and I alone.

"Do you have any idea what's on that?" Aiden asked, closing the bag of clothes I had on the bed.

"Nope." And I wasn't sure I wanted to find out.

TWENTY-FIVE

ROWAN

AIDEN AND I WERE finally home. It felt like a lifetime since I had stepped foot into this apartment. I needed to get things rolling and figure out what I was going to do with my store but first, I needed to see what the hell Miguel left for me on this USB stick.

Grabbing my laptop, I brought it out to the living room and hobbled over to the couch. I was still moving slow after getting shot. The doctors said I could have a nasty scar. I didn't care. It just added to my sparkling personality.

The pain rushing through me from being shot, reminded me that I was in fact, very much alive. As much as it hurt, I limited the pain meds I took. I was sure it wouldn't make sense to most, but I needed the pain. I needed the constant reminder that I survived.

"I'll give you some privacy."

My head snapped up. "I don't fucking think so." I grabbed Aiden's hand and pulled him down beside me. "I need you here."

When he went to argue, I grabbed his jaw. "Listen to me, you are my damn strength. You got me? I don't know what sort of sick game Miguel's playing but I need you here."

Aiden only nodded.

"Good boy." Sticking the drive into my laptop, I opened the file, but I wasn't expecting to see what came up.

"Is that…"

"It's a will and…" There was a folder marked with my name and I knew what it was before I clicked on it.

"Holy shit," Aiden whispered.

Pictures and videos came up of what I had done for Miguel and vice versa. He had saved everything. It had been a stipulation that nothing would be saved. It was to protect both of us, but he never followed through.

On my end, I had created a program that would delete photos and videos I got from the dark web. I had created it in a way that even if I tried saving anything, it wouldn't let me, and it would give my computer a nasty virus. It only happened once because I forgot about it. I learned my lesson real fast after that.

"I trusted him," I heard myself say.

Aiden placed his hand on my knee that was currently bouncing up and down. When he touched me, it stopped, a sense of calm rushing through me at the contact.

"I'm sorry," he said gently.

When I closed out of the folder with the pictures and videos, I opened the will. My eyes widened. He left everything to me. Every single fucking thing that belonged to Miguel, was mine.

"Looked like he felt guilty for keeping everything." Aiden pointed to a sentence on the screen.

He was right. It clearly said that he never followed through on what we had agreed on when we started sharing videos and pictures for money. The guilt destroyed him. That was what pushed him to come to my store in the first place.

"I'm deleting these," I said more to reassure Aiden that I wanted nothing more to do with that part of my life. After deleting the pictures and videos, I double-checked and made sure that besides the will, there was no more evidence of what Miguel and I had shared between us. But even though I did that, I would never actually know if Miguel made copies or not.

"Whatever happens, I'm here," Aiden reassured me. He grabbed my hands and lifted them to his mouth, placing soft pecks on my knuckles.

"I don't deserve you." I pulled my hand from his grasp and cupped his cheek. "But I appreciate you being here for me."

"You've done the same for me, Rowan." He cupped my hand, placing a kiss on my palm. "I love you."

A shiver raced down my spine at his words. "And I love you, Aiden. More than I could ever tell you."

EPILOGUE

AIDEN

"ARE YOU HAPPY?" ASHTON asked, taking a sip of his beer.

"I am." I smiled. "Very happy."

For the first time since I could remember, it didn't bother me that he was drinking and I wasn't. I didn't crave alcohol like I used to. It could have been because of the AA meetings I started attending more frequently but I liked to think that it mostly had to do with Rowan.

He saved me. Literally.

"How's that man of yours?"

At the mention of Rowan, a grin pulled at my lips. I couldn't help it. We had been living together for a year and dating just as long. Sure we did things a little backwards, but it worked for us.

"He's good. He's at his parents' place for dinner." I had been invited but I needed to see my brother. His wife had their baby girl a few months back, so life was busy. Even though that had been the case, we started making it a goal to hang out at least once a month. Anything more than that, was an added bonus.

"How are *you* doing?" Ashton asked, which meant, how was I dealing with things.

"I'm taking it one day at a time." Dad and I started getting along better. Mom didn't look so rundown anymore. She had a glow and Dad said that it was because of me.

I did what I could to stay away from alcohol as I didn't want to be tempted to drink but at the same time, it no longer took over my life.

AA meetings had become a weekly ritual for me. I started going to a different one at another location thanks to Rowan's parents telling me about it. I didn't see Tana again after I had thanked her. Her hitting on me back in the beginning had given me the push I needed to get out of there.

I had a new sponsor, thanks to Rowan's parents.

I hung out with friends more and was finally happy. I had told my brother that I was, but for the first time in a very long time, I didn't just say it. I felt it too.

"I've been sober, for almost a year and a half." As soon as those words left my lips, clapping erupted in the small room. "My boyfriend told me that he wants to get married on my two-year anniversary, but he hasn't proposed yet, so who knows when it comes to him. He'll probably just end up taking me to the courthouse one day instead of giving me a heads-up." I laughed at the thought. "Anyway, that's all really."

When I left the stage, the organizer of the meeting took my place. I didn't stick around like I usually did but what I liked about this group was that they never asked questions. They were just there. If I relapsed, they were there. If I stayed sober, they were there. And I couldn't thank them enough for it.

When I stepped out into the cool evening air, a shiver raced down my spine. My eyes landed on Rowan leaning against his car. His head lifted as I approached him. My feet pulled me forward, leading the way to the man that had been my undoing from the very beginning.

Before he could say anything, I closed the distance between us and pushed him up against the car. My mouth came down hard on his, pulling a groan from the back of his throat. Inching my hands beneath his shirt, I ran my palms along his abs.

"Aiden," he whispered, wrapping his arms around me.

"I just wanted to thank you," I said against his lips. I nipped and sucked at them, leaving them swollen.

"You can thank me like that anytime." He tugged me closer, pushing his pelvis into mine.

I chuckled, breaking the kiss. "Thank you, Rowan. Seriously. For everything. For loving me. For putting up with me. For just being there for me and for being patient."

"You don't have to thank me, baby boy." He leaned his forehead against mine. "But you're welcome. For everything."

"Take me home," I said, pulling away from him.

Rowan smirked, a wicked glint flashing in his eyes. "I have a better idea."

"Oh? And what's that?" I asked even though I knew that look. He was going to take me somewhere. Somewhere we had been talking about for a while now.

"Whatever happens, just know that it's you and me against the world. Always." Rowan opened the driver's side door.

"It's always been you, Rowan. No one else." I joined him and sat in the passenger seat. "But I want you to live up to your promise."

"You ready for that?" he asked, raising an eyebrow.

I leaned toward him and cupped his cheek, pressing my mouth to his ear. "I want you to fuck me in a room full of people. Where they can't do anything but watch. They're tempted to join but they aren't allowed. I want it all, Rowan. With you. Show me what you like."

"Fuck," he muttered, pulling the car out of the parking lot.

I chuckled, sitting back in my seat. "I love you."

"I love you, Aiden." He cupped my inner thigh. "And I promise to take care of you. Always." He gave my thigh a squeeze. "Now, lets go tempt some voyeurs."

BONUS SCENE

ROWAN

EVERYONE SURROUNDING US, HELD their breath.

We had never been to this club before but we made it a mission to try out as many different ones as we could together.

Aiden shook beneath me, his fists clutching the red satin sheets. He was sexy as fuck with his ass in the air and the marks from my palm on his flesh.

"Say it," I demanded.

"Fuck me," he whined.

As soon as I thrust into him, a collective sigh filled the room. It would have made me laugh if I wasn't focused on trying to make my husband fall apart in my arms.

We had been married for a month and we lived each day to its fullest. He had gained weight, continued attending AA meetings regularly, and he even got his license back. The man I was married to was nothing like the broken one I had met over two years ago.

Alcoholism was a disease that he would battle for the rest of his life but together, we would help him through it. Even if he never asked for my help, I would be there.

Later that night, we were in the room I had rented for us.

Naked and spent, we were pigging out on junk food and watching a black and white horror movie on the TV. While neither of us really knew what the movie was about, it was more background noise than anything. Just being here with Aiden was perfect.

"I never thought I'd be down for people watching me have sex," Aiden confessed, breaking the silence. "But I enjoy it. A lot."

"I know." We had come back to the room and fucked two more times before I let him be. He tried controlling me at one point which was cute, but it never worked, and I ended up taking over and pushing him to the floor. My dick still hurt from the way his teeth had scraped along it while I fucked his face.

"Rowan?"

"Hmm?" I shoved a fry into my mouth, waiting for my husband to tell me whatever it was that he wanted to say.

"Would you be down to adopt?"

My eyes snapped to his. "You want to adopt? A baby? With me?"

He nodded slowly. "If you want kids anyway. We never really talked about it, but I—"

In a quick move, I shoved him onto his back, my knees landing in the food but at that moment, I didn't care.

Aiden stared up at me with wide eyes and dilated pupils.

"Yes." I straddled his waist. "Yes, I want to adopt a baby with you. Or a kid. Or a fucking puppy. I want to adopt all the things. With you."

A bubble of laughter left him, his eyes shining. "Maybe we can start with an animal and go from there."

"Fuck that." I moved to the spot between his legs and pushed my waist into him, making his breath catch. "We're going to adopt a baby, a puppy, and a cat. Maybe even some plants. But I want to start a family with you, Aiden."

"Good."

Before I knew what was happening, Aiden had me on my back. "Do you think we're ready?"

"Are most people ready?" I cupped his face, running my finger along the scruff on his cheek.

"True." He stared down at me. "You really want to do this?"

"With you? Yes. Definitely."

A wide grin spread on his face. "When?"

"Tomorrow." I had him on his back once again. "But for now," I flipped him onto his stomach and shoved his head into the pillow. "I'm going to fuck my husband."

And for the rest of the night, I did.

THE END

The Next Generation Series:
https://www.aboutjmwalker.com/the-next-generation-series

ACKNOWLEDGEMENTS

If you're read this far, I can't thank you enough. If you would have told me 10 years ago that I would spend over 5 years writing 3 series that all involve the same characters and world, I wouldn't have believed you. This is it. Book 11 in The Next Generation Series. The series…IS DONE. I really can't thank you enough for reading, for spending time with my words, for your support and for just being the amazing person that you are.

My team: Angie, Jennifer, Christina and Joanne. Thank you for helping me through this series. Thank you for holding my hand and for giving me a push when I need it. I really can't thank you girls enough and I couldn't ask for better ladies to be at my side through this journey.

My Jems, my readers: You know who you are. You are the reason I do what I do. So, thank you.

I still can't believe that this series is done and while I'm sad this world is over, I have so many more fun ideas and some crazy books in store for you.

Early warning: I'm sorry.

J.M.

xx

ABOUT

J.M. Walker, a Canadian author, is an Amazon bestselling author who also hit USA Today with Wanted: An Outlaw Anthology and the Dissent Anthology. She loves all things books, pigs and lip gloss. She is happily married to the man who inspires all of her Heroes and continues to make her weak in the knees every single day.

"Above all, be the HEROINE of your own life..." ~ Nora Ephron

Find me!

https://linktr.ee/authorjmwalker